# THE WIFE

FOXGLOVES REGENCY ROMANCE BOOK 3

K.P. MARCH

*For those who love, work, and fight for their relationship every day. Whether with a partner, a family member, a friend, or yourself, I write this book for you.*

*And for my sister.*

# WARNING

This story does not have any trigger warnings.

The FMC is resilient and possesses a deep, quiet strength. The MMC is complex and feels things deeply. They are both flawed, struggle to navigate their emotions, and make mistakes, but they take accountability for themselves, their actions, and their impact.

This is a standalone book in an interconnected series. Guaranteed HEA. You will see Anna and Charles again as side characters in future books.

# THE FOXGLOVES CIRCLE

*Amelia Edwards / Amelia Becham*
    Duchess of Birmingham
    Gideon Edwards's wife
    Lydia Colbrook's sister
    Thomas Colbrook's childhood friend

*Lydia Colbrook / Lydia Becham*
    Countess of Coventry
    Thomas Colbrook's wife
    Amelia Edwards's sister

*Thomas Colbrook*
    Earl of Coventry
    Lydia Colbrook's husband
    Amelia Edwards's childhood friend

*Emily Davenport*
    Jack and Grace Davenport's sister
    Anna Lucas's childhood friend

*Grace Davenport*
　　Jack and Emily Davenport's sister

*Jack Davenport*
　　Emily and Grace Davenport's brother
　　Alexander Vaughton's childhood friend

*Genevieve Sinclair / Lady Genevieve Edwards*
　　Daughter of the late Duke and Duchess of Birmingham
　　Oliver Sinclair's wife
　　Gideon Edwards's sister

*Gideon Edwards*
　　The Duke of Birmingham
　　Amelia Edwards's husband
　　Genevieve Sinclair's brother

*Lady Anna Lucas*
　　Daughter of the Earl and Countess of Dunhill
　　Charles Sinclair's fiancée
　　Emily Davenport's childhood friend

*Philip Mason*
　　Viscount of St. Alsbrook

*Charles Sinclair*
　　Anna Lucas's fiancée
　　Oliver Sinclair's brother

*Oliver Sinclair*
　　Genevieve Sinclair's husband
　　Charles Sinclair's brother

*Alexander Vaughton*
    Marquess of Ronan
    Jack Davenport's childhood friend

# THE FOXGLOVES CHILDREN

Thomas and Lydia Colbrook:
*Adelaide Colbrook*, ~November 1808
*John Colbrook*, ~November 1809

Gideon and Amelia Edwards:
*George Edwards*, ~January 1809
*Guinevere Edwards*, ~December 1809
*\*Expected*, Spring 1811

Oliver and Genevieve Sinclair:
*\*Expected*, Spring 1811

# CHAPTER 1

## ANNA

1810, LONDON, ENGLAND

*A*nna sat by the window in the Dunhill House drawing room, holding a book open in her hands. She'd barely read more than a handful of words over the past hour, however, as her gaze fixed itself instead on the London streets. She observed the people coming and going, strolling arm in arm, talking and laughing gaily as they enjoyed their final days in Town.

The Season was over. In another week, she and her parents, the Earl and Countess of Dunhill, would depart their Town-home in favor of their country estate like the rest of the *ton*. But unlike them, Anna's stay at her family's country home would not last until next Season.

No, for Anna Lucas, her days at her childhood home were numbered. She would stay there for only these final few months before she married and left it for good.

As if to remind her of that very fact, she was pulled from her examination of passersby by her mother's entrance into the drawing room. Anna was a very near copy of the beautiful and graceful Daphne Lucas, only her mother had the lines and sparkles of gray hair that Anna would not match for a few decades yet.

"There you are, Anna darling," her mother said. "We must be going. Your dress is ready."

Her wedding dress.

"Of course, Mother," Anna replied, standing without protest. Her words and demeanor belied the heaviness of her thoughts.

She placed her book on one of the many tables nestled about the room, all topped with the endless arrangements of flowers her mother always insisted upon maintaining. Anna loved the colors, scents, and breathtaking beauty her mother crammed into their Townhouse. The result gave the room the calming effect of a wondrous garden, rather than seeming ridiculous in its abundance of never-ending flowers.

What's more, to Anna, the flowers felt like life, like hope. With their delicate beauty, one would think them incapable of withstanding the harshness of nature, and yet, they thrived within it. Resilient. Uplifting. A reminder that even during your most troubling times, life persisted. No matter how weak it may look, that flower drank in the storm and *bloomed*.

Which was why after she placed her unread book on the nearest table, she trailed a finger along the soft petals of one of the lovely foxgloves showcased in the current arrangements. The tall, vibrant bloom with its bell-shaped flowers had recently become her favorite.

"Come, dear," her mother interrupted Anna's dawdling.

Without a word, Anna followed her mother out of the house and into the carriage. As they traveled, the first few moments passed in silence, and Anna once again watched the London streets as they rode through them. She hadn't realized how quiet she had become, however, until her mother spoke.

"Is something troubling you, Anna?" Her mother's kind voice interrupted her reverie again.

Anna turned to meet her worried green eyes, the only thing she had not inherited from her.

"Not at all, Mother," Anna lied smoothly and unnecessarily.

Because they both knew what Anna thought about day in and day out. Her impending nuptials had been consuming all of Anna's waking thoughts for weeks now. Ever since the wedding of her future brother-in-law, Oliver Sinclair, and her good friend, Genevieve Edwards, now Genevieve Sinclair. She would have thought the newlywed's relationship, potential scandal, and quick wedding would be a welcome distraction. Instead of taking the attention away from her own upcoming marriage to Charles Sinclair, however, it threw an obvious light on it by its sheer proximity. Anna had been included in all the planning and preparations for Genevieve's wedding as any close family member would. And now that Genevieve and Oliver were happily married – and already expecting their first child – all their friends and family had shifted their attentions to the next soon-to-be-wed couple.

In truth, Anna was thrilled about Genevieve's marriage to Oliver. It meant she would now have a sister and companion within her new family. Anna and Charles had been engaged for as long as she could remember. Truly. It had been decided when Anna was two and Charles was ten. That was when Albert Lucas, the Earl of Dunhill and Anna's father, had made a poor and volatile investment that emptied the Dunhill coffers of everything they'd held. They were saved by his friend, the man that had advised Albert *not* to make such a reckless and life-altering investment, Walter Sinclair.

Walter had been an exceedingly kind, intelligent, and rich business tycoon, but the one thing he lacked was a title. So, he proposed an alliance to serve both families – his oldest son, Charles, and the Dunhill's only child, Anna, would marry when she reached the age of twenty. The Sinclairs would provide the Lucases with much needed funds and guidance on investments to grow their money; the Lucases would provide the Sinclairs with an earl in their lineage. It was easily fixed and solved, and everyone was happy about it.

Except Anna and Charles.

As the young, betrothed couple grew up, the two held their responsibility in the highest regard. They treated each other with politeness and understood the necessity of their engagement. Neither one of them even considered breaking it. But neither did they grow close. Their families, especially in recent years, this past one in particular, had tried to shove the pair together at every opportunity. Even creating opportunities where none existed to force them to start building a relationship. The result, however, was their polite participation... and silence. They performed. They danced. They sat together. They walked arm in arm. But beyond the required courtesies of a greeting and farewell, Anna and Charles did not speak.

It bothered Anna. It always did. She knew Charles was a good man. Good and kind and terribly handsome. But she never knew how to connect with him. Not even how to begin trying. She had no idea how to bridge the lifelong distance that existed between them, and it was a struggle that she had contemplated many times over the years. She was just as much to blame, of course. For each step he didn't take in her direction, she never took one in his. But it had always felt like she had more time.

She knew her time had run out, though, as the carriage pulled to a stop outside the dressmaker's shop. Her completed wedding gown waited inside, wrapped and ready to be taken home. She stepped out of the carriage knowing there was no escape.

# CHAPTER 2

## CHARLES

"Charles, it's a lovely day today," Prudence Sinclair said over breakfast in the Sinclair House dining room. She eyed him where he sat next to her at the head of the table, her baby blue eyes twinkling and assessing. Light streaming in from the large arched windows behind her lit up the pale blue wallpaper like the sky outside, emphasizing her point.

"It is, Mother," he muttered, sparing her a glance before taking another bite of his scone. He knew what she suggested. Or rather, what she was about to suggest. And she also knew his reply. His brother and sister-in-law watched knowingly, too, from beside each other on his other side. Why they all bothered with the charade, he didn't know.

"I am sure Anna would enjoy a carriage ride or walk in the park on such a beautiful day," his mother continued in her shamelessly cheerful tone that did little to cover up the expectation lying heavily beneath it.

"I am sure she would," he replied noncommittally, reaching for his tea to keep his hands and mouth busy.

His mother's answering sigh felt over the top, even for her.

"Why do you insist on being so unnecessarily stubborn, my dear? I do wish you'd stop."

"I am not being stubborn," Charles answered in a dry tone.

"What I think she's trying to say," his new sister, Genevieve, cut the tension in her high, sweet voice from his left. Her dark hair was loose, and she watched him with matching dark eyes. "Is perhaps *you* could take Anna for a ride today."

"He knows exactly what I'm saying," his mother said in the simultaneously bright and disappointed voice only she could really manage.

"He's just choosing to behave like a fool," Oliver contributed with a shake of his head. Charles's younger brother's careless brown hair and groomed beard were perfectly styled, and he did not bother lifting his dark blue eyes from his plate as he spoke.

"I know," Genevieve replied softly.

Charles ignored them all, picking up his fork and resuming his breakfast. He could feel his family's expectations circling around him. Luckily, he was skilled at maintaining his cool. Any other individual would have likely blushed in shame under the collective weight of their judgment; Charles, on the other hand, kept his back straight and head high.

"What are you doing, Charles?" Oliver finally sighed, reaching his hand mindlessly over to rub his wife's back, either to comfort her or himself in their mutual frustration, Charles wasn't sure, but he did not appreciate seeing it.

Not that he begrudged either Oliver or Genevieve their relationship. Those two deserved each other and every happiness in the world. There had been a moment when Charles thought his brother would be too foolish to seize the love of, almost quite literally, his entire life, but they sorted themselves out right enough. And now Charles would soon have a niece or nephew, which he could not have been happier about.

But still, must they flaunt how perfectly soul mated they

were and had always been when discussing the wife that had been thrust upon him?

And, he petulantly continued in his own mind – because he would only be this rude and unreasonable within the safety of his private thoughts – why should they be so frustrated and in need of comfort over *his* marriage?

Of course, he knew it was because they cared and loved both him and Anna. That was why they didn't leave him alone, and that was also why he would never say such ridiculous and selfish thoughts out loud to anyone.

"Take Lady Anna out today," his brother continued, hand still rubbing Genevieve's back lovingly. "We're only in Town for another four days, and this is your last chance before the wedding. Don't waste it."

"I will see her tomorrow night," Charles reminded them. He knew what they meant, though. He could, and *should*, call on her. Tomorrow night was a formal dinner at Coventry House. It wasn't a final opportunity to court his wife like today would be.

But Charles had no interest in courting her. He was already marrying her. What purpose *was* there to courting her?

"Charles, you are cutting off your nose to spite your face, dear," his mother spoke. "I want two happy daughters. Must you insist on denying me that?"

"I am doing no such thing, Mother," he paused to take another sip of tea, hoping it would calm the familiar lifelong emotions roiling through him, like the rocky waves of an ocean storm. These were always the feelings that accompanied thoughts of his marriage. A marriage that had been decided for him when he was a child barely able to understand the concept. And Anna, as innocent as she was in the whole mess, was the embodiment of that. Why would he spend time with her when all it would do would be to keep the waves of unease and turmoil rocketing through his chest the entire time?

"Anna is a perfectly happy person," he continued, placing the delicate cup back down, the contents almost fully drained, and still the feelings crashed through him. Outwardly, he did not waver. He never did. "I would never do anything to take that from her or hurt her."

He meant that. He would never harm his wife. Ever. Of course, he wouldn't.

Genevieve bit her lip, hesitating before being the one to reply. "Neglect is also painful, Charles," Genevieve spoke with such care and kindness, Charles instinctively felt himself bracing. "I know you do not mean to cause her pain, nor does she you, but perhaps you could both consider that whatever is driving you to hold yourselves apart also causes you to hurt one another, unintentional as it may be."

The waves of his emotions crashed harder within him, almost making it noticeable to his companions how he lost his breath.

But what else could he do? Charles could not handle the whirlpool of contradicting, overpowering emotions inside himself when he was near Anna. She was the reminder of a life's worth of stolen choices, not just in the choice of bride. It was unfair, he knew that, wildly and irrationally unfair. But as he'd grown up, it was as if all the responsibilities, expectations, stolen freedoms that he took in stride suddenly concentrated and turned to bitterness when he approached his marriage – the most profound choice that had been robbed from him.

He didn't know how to confront his feelings, confront *her*. He didn't know *how* to speak to her. This was not Charles. He knew how to speak, he knew how to keep a hold on himself, he knew how to maintain a cool and level-head at all times.

Except where his wife was concerned.

"If you'll excuse me," he stood from the table. "There are matters requiring my attention."

"Anna needs your attention," Oliver accurately called him out.

Charles met his brother's eyes with a cool gaze, but the war still raged on the stormy waves within him. He wanted to do right by Anna. He did. But he didn't want to reminded of all these choices he never got to make. He didn't want to feel this bitterness, this confusion, this madness.

So, he left the table without another word.

Because what was the point? There was no escape.

# CHAPTER 3

## ANNA

*A*nna was the last to arrive at Birmingham House for tea. Lewis, the Duke and Duchess of Birmingham's butler, led her through the large and open Townhouse with its warm woods and brightness. None of their homes, Anna's own included, would be considered small or humble, but the Birmingham's was by far the most extravagant and yet also the most welcoming.

"Lady Anna, Your Grace," Lewis announced her as she entered the drawing room. The heavy curtains were parted, letting in the overcast light through the room's large windows. The blue wallpaper looked gray and comforting in the cozy glow of the dreary afternoon.

The ladies were already seated on the richly embroidered sofas arranged before the fireplace. Their hostess, Amelia Edwards, the Duchess of Birmingham and Genevieve's sister-in-law, occupied one couch with her sister, Lydia Colbrook, the Countess of Coventry, and Genevieve. Anna moved to join her oldest friend, Emily Davenport, and her sister, Grace, on the sofa opposite them as she greeted everyone.

"So, what were you discussing before I arrived?" Anna asked, taking the cup Amelia poured for her from the tray on the small center table.

These afternoon teas had become something of a tradition for their group over the past two years, through which the women had built and strengthened a true friendship with one another. Anna and Emily had been friends almost their whole lives, having grown up near each other. Two years ago, during Emily's first Season, they made the acquaintance of, then, Amelia and Lydia Becham. Genevieve had joined their group last year when Amelia insisted her husband, Gideon Edwards, the Duke of Birmingham, and his younger sister, Genevieve, join the Season in London, even though Genevieve had not yet come out. Similarly, Grace had joined their circle this year, though she was set to debut the following year.

The ladies met for tea at least every other week during the Season and supported each other unfailingly through life in a way their husbands could not. Anna knew, of course, that Amelia, Lydia, and Genevieve were all three very lucky and happy in their marriages, but the bond these women shared was different from those they held with the men in their lives.

Anna sat back with the delicate teacup held gently between her fingers. She took a sip of the warm liquid while looking expectantly over its rim at her friends.

"Emily's prospects," Genevieve supplied. "She's still convinced she is destined for a life of spinsterhood."

"Oh, Em," Anna sighed, placing her cup back on the saucer and turning to her friend. "You know that's simply not true."

"It is," Emily rolled her eyes. "I don't know why you all must insist otherwise. Some of us find our matches, some of us don't. It's just the way of things." She didn't sound resigned or defeated; rather, Emily spoke in her usual vibrant, happy voice.

"I think you will find a husband, sister," Grace replied in a delicate, demure voice completely unlike her sister's. The two women looked almost unrelated when seen without their brother to bridge the resemblance between them. Both beautiful, Emily's eyes were caramel, her hair dark, where Grace's eyes were hazel and hair golden. They were opposite not only in looks, but also in demeanor. Emily was boisterous and bright, where Grace was reserved and proud. Perhaps she had to be with Emily having taken up their entire family's share of enthusiasm with her magnetic personality.

"What about Mr. Thompson?" Amelia asked in her unusually husky, feminine voice after the single dance partner Emily had that Season who was not one of their own circle of friends.

Amelia was also expecting, about a month behind Genevieve. Neither woman showed yet, and Anna thought it was quite sweet that the two cousins would be practically twins upon their birth. Amelia and Gideon already had an almost two-year-old son, George, and an almost one-year-old daughter, Guinevere. Lydia and her husband, Thomas Colbrook, the Earl of Coventry, had two children of about the same age, as well, Adelaide and her younger brother, John.

Emily chuckled. "Poor Mr. Thompson. I do feel sorry that he had to dance with me."

"Why should you feel sorry?" Anna inquired, her brows pinching slightly at Emily's words.

"Anna, you know perfectly well the only reason he asked me to dance was because *you* made him. That poor gentleman only stopped to have a drink of punch and then you cornered him into dancing with me."

"I did not *corner* him." She absolutely had. "I simply drew his attention to how lovely you looked that evening as you do *all* evenings. Why should you feel sorry for a gentleman getting to dance with a beautiful lady?"

"My goodness, the way you twist things," Emily finally scowled at her.

Anna merely shrugged, completely unapologetic and in the right. It was that Thompson's lucky day to get to dance with

Emily Davenport. Her friend was the best person in all the world, and Anna would die in that fight without hesitation.

"She's completely right, Emily," Lydia replied, her angelic face with blonde hair and blue eyes looked at their friend as if she missed the obvious. "You should not feel sorry for a man's good fortune in spending the evening with you."

"That's just further proof," Emily gestured with her teacup, careful not to spill its contents. "He did *not* spend the evening with me. Nor did he call on me afterwards."

"All the more his loss and foolishness," Anna muttered into her cup.

"Oh, ladies," Emily finished taking a sip. "One day you will realize I am right. It is simply not my lot to find a husband. And that is perfectly alright. I will spend my days surrounded by my friends and your beautiful children. All I ask is you keep me in fresh and abundant supply of them so that I may be their overindulgent Aunt Emily."

Anna disagreed vehemently, but she held her tongue. She knew her friend well and could see that she truly believed in what she said. No amount of arguing would make Emily see otherwise, and she genuinely would be happy in such a life. Emily was just that sort of person. She was the embodiment of happiness and love and life. But she deserved more than what she would cheerfully settle for. She deserved the husband she had always wanted since they were little girls.

No, if Anna wanted to make a difference on Emily's outlook, she and their friends would have to scheme elsewhere. They'd have to make these foolish, blind men of the *ton* see the wonder that was Emily. Once they did, she wouldn't be able to fight them off, there would be so many. And Anna would *make* it happen. For Emily and her friends, she would make *anything* happen.

"Have you heard from Charles at all, Anna?" Amelia asked, also clearly sensing the topic of Emily's prospects exhausted for the time being. Anna looked over at her friend, who had soft brown eyes, dark gold hair, and features that very strongly resembled her younger sister's.

She sighed quietly through her nose, reflexively ensuring no one noticed. Of course, she knew this topic would make its way to centerstage over the course of the afternoon.

"Not since the ball last week," she answered honestly. It had been the final ball of the Season, and Charles had danced with her more than once. Three times, to be exact. He'd been doing that more and more since around Oliver and Genevieve's wedding.

In fact, throughout the Season, there had been several moments where things felt... different. The extra dances. How he'd called her beautiful for the first time in their lives. She always thought he didn't consider her to be, and to hear him say otherwise had made her heart glow.

Then, there was the way he'd watched her when she walked down the aisle at his brother's wedding. She still thought about that moment often. Walking towards him, foxgloves clutched in her hands, and Charles looking at her with such wonder painted across his face. It had felt like a dream. The best dream she would never allow herself to imagine. And now, she could no longer look at a foxglove without remembering her husband's eyes on her. Watching her like she was all he could ever want from life.

Yet, even with all that, her fiancée still barely spoke to her.

"That is difficult," Amelia said in a frustrated tone, shaking her head as she stirred her tea more out of annoyance than in an effort to cool it.

Anna's eye landed on Genevieve as she took another sip of her tea. Her future sister-in-law looked pensive but said nothing, which was not uncommon. She and Grace were the quietest of their group.

"Is everything alright, Genevieve?" Anna asked.

Genevieve's heavy gaze lifted to Anna before she answered evenly, "Of course."

"Genevieve mentioned before you arrived that she, Oliver, and Prudence urged Charles to call on you yesterday. You know, one last time before we all left London," Emily supplied as she placed her empty teacup down on the table. She leaned back, opening her fan and gently cooling her face. "Clearly, he did not agree."

"Clearly," Anna repeated, nodding. She held her back straight and chin up, showing no outward indication of how her chest hollowed out at the realization that Charles had, yet again, chosen not to see her.

"We are worried about you," Genevieve said quietly.

Anna wasn't sure if the 'we' meant the women present or the Sinclairs, or both.

Regardless, Anna reassured them in a steady voice, "I do not believe there is anything to particularly worry over. All is as it should be, as I keep telling you. We are civil to one another. Perform our duties by each other well, and I am confident we will continue to do so as husband and wife. Our wedding is set, and we will soon assume our new roles."

"Goodness, that sounds...," Grace's musical voice trailed off.

"Anna," Lydia said soothingly. "That's precisely why we are worried. We do not want for you both to 'assume roles' with regard to one another. Even if you have in the past, that's not what your marriage should be. We want you to be with each other as you are with no one else. You will be the other half of each other's lives. That is not a *role*. It's becoming whole."

Anna's heart ricocheted at Lydia's words. How wonderful that would be, what she described, but it would not be the reality for her. "Charles and I, I believe, have an understanding," Anna offered, her voice unwavering even as her heart fluttered.

"How can you have an understanding if you do not even

speak to one another?" Genevieve challenged gently, encouraging Anna to assess her own evasiveness.

It was true. Their entire group, women and men, had been creating opportunities for the couple to interact, spend time together, talk. None of it worked, but their efforts had been both coordinated and fully transparent. The lack of success only disheartened Anna further. Regardless of the odd moments this Season that could have been more, it was unmistakably apparent that Charles truly did not want her or their marriage. He never even asked how she was. He did nothing to create actual closeness between them. Rather, he made the line between them distinct and clear, and he upheld it diligently.

"You don't always need to speak to communicate," Anna told Genevieve the truth.

The room fell silent for a beat. Anna finished the last of her tea, placing the cup back on the table before them. She assumed her friends were finally starting to realize what she already knew – love or even friendship between her and Charles was a lost cause.

"Why have you been so troubled, then, if you have this understanding?" Grace broke the silence, her voice genuine.

"That's right," Emily picked up the thought with animation. "All through Genevieve and Oliver's wedding planning, all through *your* wedding planning, all through the Season. You have been solemn and withdrawn, and admitted to being troubled. Why, then?"

Anna swallowed, her first outward indication of the sadness that coursed through her when she considered Charles and the depth of his disregard. If the ladies noticed, she didn't know, but Anna kept her voice and countenance steady. "All humans want love, where possible, and I am no exception. So, yes, it does trouble me that love is not possible in my marriage, but that does not mean it will be a bad one. Charles is a good man, you all know it," she looked around the group, not acknowledging the sympathy, perhaps pity, in their gazes. "And he will take care of me. He will be a good husband, and I a good wife. There are many out there far less fortunate, particularly in circumstances like ours. I understand the kind of marriage I will have, and I accept it." Then, she said the honest thing she had not yet voiced, but finally felt she had to. For her own sanity, she had to. "I no longer want to keep fighting it. I know you all mean well, as do the gentleman, but nothing will change. Nothing *has* changed. Not really. And I am tired of all the efforts to make my relationship something it is not."

"We understand, darling," Lydia said. "But let us try just once more. Tonight, you are all coming for dinner. Let us try to encourage something more between you and hope that Charles does respond. But you must try, too. *Really* try. It is not only he who holds himself apart. If nothing changes, we will not push you two together anymore. Not leading up to the wedding, at the wedding, or during your marriage. We will support you, and if you say you want us to stop, we will stop. But let us try in true earnest this one time."

Anna inhaled deeply, only obvious in the slight over-expansion of her chest, and breathed back out before she agreed. "Just tonight. In truth. But then, no more."

# CHAPTER 4

## CHARLES

The carriage slowed to a stop outside of Coventry House. The silence between Oliver, Genevieve, and him throughout their journey had felt weighted, but perhaps that was his own imagination. He felt the air around them saturated with his brother and sister-in-law's disappointment, judgment, and pressure to make the most of the evening, but logically, he knew that was unfair. They hadn't broached the subject of Anna and his relationship since yesterday's breakfast. It was equally likely they were giving him the space he had indirectly, but very obviously, asked for. Or maybe they were simply thinking their own thoughts about other things.

Fuck, he was being ridiculous.

A footman opened the door, and they exited the carriage without delay, Charles's anxiety ratcheting up with each step they took towards the front door.

"Good evening," Hughes greeted them when they entered. While Oliver attended to his wife's cloak, Charles looked around. He wasn't sure what he searched for or why his eyes wanted to wander. He'd been here many times before and knew the cheerful, tastefully luxurious Coventry House decently well.

Still, his eyes catalogued the entryway, his ears perking up for sounds of their dinner party.

Hughes led them to the drawing room, where their hosts, Thomas and Lydia Colbrook, the Earl and Countess of Coventry, already waited with the Duke and Duchess of Birmingham, the family members the Coventry's shared with his own sister-in-law, Genevieve. Before Hughes had even finished announcing them, Genevieve was across the room, Oliver beside her, greeting her brother, Gideon, as Oliver greeted Amelia. Charles crossed the fine room with its light colors and country paintings towards Thomas, who stood by the mantle.

"Welcome, Sinclair," Thomas shook his hand before they were joined by Gideon and Oliver. "We are still waiting for the rest of our guests, as you can see, before dinner is called."

The men stood in a loose semicircle facing the ladies. Lydia and Amelia resumed their seats on the cream-colored sofa, Genevieve joining them.

"Will everyone be in attendance?" Oliver asked from beside the duke.

"Indeed," Thomas replied.

His wife completed the thought. "The Viscount of St. Alsbrook, the Marquess of Ronan, and the Davenports, who will also be escorting Anna tonight, I believe," Lydia confirmed.

Charles did not let on how his heart stuttered at his wife's name. He didn't particularly like another man, a longtime family friend though Jack Davenport may be, escorting her anywhere, even if it was within their own circle.

He breathed through it, unwilling to examine the feeling.

As if he'd summoned them, Hughes entered once again and announced, "Mr. Davenport, Miss Davenport, Miss Grace, and Lady Anna."

Jack Davenport was a tall, decent-looking man, and a mix of his two lovely sisters flanking him. He had the same brown, wavy hair of one, and the striking hazel eyes of the other.

But Charles only vaguely registered the Davenport family as they entered the drawing room. No, his attention focused wholly on his wife, as it always did when she was in the same room. Their friends and family all thought he didn't pay any attention to her, and based on outward appearances, they would be correct. But the truth was that the minute Anna was in his vicinity, everything else ceased to exist for Charles. It had always been that way, even when he was a little boy and she was barely a little girl. Back then, it had been an awareness of being connected to this child when he was also a child, but these past few years, it had become something more obsessive than that.

And he hadn't the faintest idea how to navigate the change.

So, he barely looked at her as she walked into the room, smiling as she greeted the ladies and joked quietly at seeing each other again so soon. He knew Genevieve saw her today at tea, even if he hadn't asked after it.

"Gentlemen," Jack greeted them pleasantly, taking up a position beside Charles. "I hope we have not kept you waiting."

"Not at all," Thomas said cheerfully. Charles had never met a more genuinely happy person than Thomas Colbrook. He even *looked* cheerful with his unrelentingly jovial face, light hair, and light eyes. "You are right on time. And we are still awaiting St. Alsbrook and Ronan."

Charles let the conversation buzz around him as he pretended not to notice Anna in her garnet red dress. He would have thought the color would clash with the shining red hair piled exquisitely atop her head, highlighting her long, delicate neck decorated with jewels; but somehow, it complemented it perfectly. He'd yet to see her wear anything that did not look splendid on her and her petite frame. She was the perfect size to envelope in his arms, not that he ever tried. Just as he never acknowledged how, over the past few years, his wife had become his every fantasy come to life with her slim, small figure, the sweet swell of her breasts, and her delicately grabable hips.

Then, there was her face. It was indescribable, to the point that he sometimes considered her impossible to be real. Those sharp, crystal blue eyes angled up, surrounded by long, dark lashes and her arched dark red brows. Her button nose, defined cheekbones, and diamond face were scattered with hundreds upon hundreds of freckles that, rather than detract from the ethereal quality of her features, enhanced it. Both her top and bottom lips were wide and temptingly full, and naturally pulled up at the corners as if always ready to smile.

The truth was, even when they were children, Anna had not seemed real. And the way she had only grown further into that as a woman.... It crushed something within Charles, though he could not properly explain why. Only that he found it difficult to believe she could possibly be his.

"How are your impending fatherhoods?" Jack asked as Charles focused once again on his companions.

"I am already a father," Gideon replied, his green eyes amused. He and his sister looked so much alike in their features and dark hair, yet their eyes were very strikingly different. "But in answer to the essence of your question, quite well." The duke smirked.

"Oliver is not, though," Thomas said, looking at Charles's brother. Oliver, however, had his eyes fixed to his wife, a look of immense adoration sketched all over his features.

"This one is quite lost to us at the thought of it," Gideon gave a rare full smile and smacked his brother-in-law good-naturedly on the back.

"And I make no apology for it," Oliver admitted, giving them half a smile. He looked over at Genevieve again, and Charles followed his gaze to see his sister-in-law wink at her husband, a sly smile stretched across her face.

"Well, I am glad to hear it," Jack smiled both politely and genuinely.

Just then Philip Mason, the Viscount of St. Alsbrook, and Alexander Vaughton, the Marquess of Ronan, were shown into the drawing room. Philip, Alexander, Jack, and the youngest Davenport, Grace, were newer to their circle of companions, but they fit in seamlessly. Clearly, since what brought the newcomers into their group was their friends enlisting their efforts to bring Charles and Anna together these past months. Even so, as he continued to talk and laugh while waiting for dinner, Charles quite appreciated counting them all amongst his now considerable list of over-involved friends.

# CHAPTER 5

## ANNA

For the most part, Anna enjoyed the start to their evening. Mostly because she loved spending time with her close friends. She had realized some weeks ago, after the third or fourth get together this Season, that this group of people had all built their own web of affection together. They would grow old with each other, hold private dinner parties and luncheons and park outings together. Raise their children together. As she sat in the armchair, listening to her companions talk around her, the thought of her children truly brought her the contentment she had assured the ladies of earlier.

She may not be excited for her marriage, but Anna could not wait to have children.

The room overflowed with pleasant chatter and laughter of multiple conversations occurring simultaneously before it was time to make their way to the dining room.

Her companions began splitting into their usual pairs, Philip escorting Emily as he often did lately, and Jack escorting Grace.

Anna observed the genuine smile on Emily's face as she joked with the viscount, and their conversation from that afternoon played over in her mind. Her friend was so exceptional, Anna wanted the world and more for her. She sat lost to her own determined wonderings when she felt Charles's presence beside her. Looking up at him, her heart began to ache.

Charles Sinclair was so simply and devastatingly handsome. He took so much after his mother, the same incredibly light blue eyes and shining blonde hair. Even his inherently masculine features had a delicate, aristocratic cut to them like Prudence's. The arch of his brows, the strike of his nose and thin lips, the angle of his cheekbones, and the sharpness of his strong jawline. It was so precise, so fine, she wanted so much to trace each detail with her fingertips. Memorize their shape. Worship their beauty.

Charles had always seemed that way to her, even when she was young. He had always been the most beautiful person she'd ever seen. Now, grown, he was tall, broad-shouldered, his body lean and strong in a way that satisfied something deeply feminine within her.

But to have such a beautiful, strong, intelligent, refined man as one's husband and know he did not and would never want you…. It created an echo in her hollow chest.

Charles didn't speak to her. She was aware, had been since she came in tonight, that he hadn't even greeted her. There wasn't much opportunity, Anna recognized that, but looking up at him now, silent and waiting for her, she was disheartened by the continued wordlessness.

She stood and wrapped her arm around his, feeling the hard muscles of his forearm beneath her fingertips and his rich clothing. As they followed the others out of the drawing room, she took a deep inhale of the comforting forest scent that was Charles. That scent was most likely her favorite smell in the world. She wanted to wrap and burrow herself within its warmth.

She wished he would speak to her as they walked. Anna

didn't hear much of his voice, but it was like his scent – smooth, deep, comforting.

But he didn't speak.

And neither did she.

Entering the dining room, she decided to keep her word from this afternoon. She would stop holding herself apart, too, as was her instinct, and try instead. Their friends were right. This *was* their last evening together. The next time they'd see him, it would be for their wedding festivities.

Charles pulled out her chair for her before taking his place in the one beside it. The light of the several candles glittered off the crystal glasses and finely detailed china in the bright room. Three small, colorful flower arrangements alternated between the candelabras set at the center of the table with its white tablecloth. The conversation was steady around them, but Anna was conscious of more than one person's awareness on her and Charles. She was reminded that it wasn't just the women that worried about them as she surreptitiously noticed each man present casting a glance ranging from curious to concerned in their direction.

Anna gathered her courage and fortitude while they were served soup and prepared to bridge the distance between her and her fiancée for once. Picking up her spoon, she turned to Charles.

"How are you this evening, Charles?" she asked politely.

If she thought their friends were paying attention to them before, it was nothing compared to the focus she felt on her now after her six simple words. Her female companions, bless them, swiftly shifted the attention away, however, and she was grateful for it as Charles glanced at her, brows very slightly pinching.

He cleared his throat gently, focusing on his own soup as he answered quietly, "I am quite well, thank you."

That was it.

She stared at him for a beat, waiting for him to return the question, before she resumed her own meal as if everything was perfectly normal.

"And your mother?" she tried again after a moment or two passed and he made no reciprocating attempt at conversation or polite interest.

"She is also well."

Anna felt a brittleness taking hold inside her. Her palms began to sweat.

But she kept trying. She had promised she would, and if he wasn't taking a step towards her, she could take steps towards him before her steps to the altar. This was it. There was no more time after this.

"I am glad to hear it," she replied warmly. "I do admire her."

Charles made no verbal reply but gave an imperceptible nod. Apart from that first glance, he hadn't even turned his head towards her or looked at her at all, his face once again schooled in impassivity. As she observed him, she thought she recognized a slight tension around his mouth and in the way he held himself.

Turning back to her soup, Anna placed her spoon down gently and reached for her water. She swallowed the cool liquid and, with it, the fragility making her feel weak and like giving up. No, she would be strong and see this through.

Putting down her cup, she kept a pleasantly cool expression on her face as she took another few sips of her soup. Then, she turned towards him again, sure now that the tension across his features was from her attentions as she watched them thin ever so slightly more.

"How did you find this Season?" she asked in a confident and politely curious voice.

"Quite enjoyable," he answered, his words more clipped this time as he still did not look at her.

That's when she noticed how quiet the rest of the table had

become. With their large, yet intimate group, conversation was easy, organic, loud, often breaking off into smaller discussions that looped back to larger ones. Right now, however, no one spoke. Even the women had their eyes trained on Anna and Charles, their earlier consideration to keep attention off the couple giving way to what looked predominantly like shock and embarrassment from their expressions.

Anna met a few of the pitying – or were those angry? – gazes around the table before her own fixed to her bowl as shame crashed over her in a tidal wave. She was mortified. Absolutely and thoroughly mortified at the spectacle she'd just inadvertently made.

She forced her hand to keep a firm grip on her spoon, not allowing it to shake. She lifted it back to her lips, drank her soup, and ate her meal.

And did not speak another word.

# CHAPTER 6

## CHARLES

*C*harles wanted this night to be over. Normally, he enjoyed evenings with his friends, and it had started the same as any other. Of course, there was the awareness and tension between him and Anna, but the two of them had their rhythm.

Except tonight, for whatever reason, Anna had decided to disrupt it.

What was she doing? She never asked him questions, let alone continued to after he very obviously conveyed his discomfort. Why would she do that? They had their situation in hand, why was she changing things? And what in God's name was *he* doing?

He didn't know what to do. How to handle the shift in their interactions. How to withstand the tsunami within him as she kept pushing. Pushing and pushing and pushing. He felt lost and unsure – both uncommon and unwelcome feelings. So, he instinctively did his best to return them to their usual distance.

Charles focused on those thoughts. The self-defense and need for safety that spurred his behavior. Because if he didn't center all of his focus on that, he'd be seized by the guilt and regret waiting just at the edges, ready to overtake him the moment he stopped.

She didn't try speaking to him again for the rest of the painfully long dinner. Of course, he'd been aware of the very noticeable lull in conversation around the table before she did so, but since then, it had awkwardly picked back up.

Anna didn't contribute, however.

And neither did he.

At last, the ladies stood up and excused themselves for the drawing room, and the tempestuous emotions crashing through his chest finally calmed slightly with Anna's exit. Not before he caught a whiff of her delicately floral scent as she walked around him, though.

The men were served their brandy and cigars, but once the relief from the dinner ending subsided somewhat, he registered the stern expressions of his companions. None of them said anything or looked at him. In fact, if he was not mistaken, each and every one of them looked furious. Even, Philip and Thomas, who Charles would have believed incapable of the emotion.

Charles did not break the silence. He took a sip of his brandy, letting it calm the last of the violent waves within him, before he relaxed back in his chair and puffed on his cigar.

"Why did you do that?" It was Alexander who put the question to him, his voice hard and demanding. The Marquess of Ronan was an impressively intimidating man, the most severe of their group, with dark hair and sharp gray eyes.

Charles could deny it, but he was no fool, and neither were the men around him. They all knew what he had done.

He had humiliated her.

"I don't know how to speak to her," he replied honestly, his voice steady.

"Bullshit," both Gideon and Oliver said, the latter with more ire.

Charles sighed and dropped his head into his free hand,

rubbing at his forehead while his cigar hand reached for his glass again.

"You know how to make conversation, even the most insincere and rudimentary of them," Thomas spoke, his voice marginally softer than the others', but his expression just as severe. "What you did was intentional."

Charles tossed back the entirety of his glass, hoping the burn through his chest would distract him from the oppressive guilt his friends were dragging to the forefront of his mind.

"I don't believe I have ever witnessed a gentleman treat a lady like that," Philip added, shaking his dark blonde head. His blue eyes watched him with a mixture of disappointment and disgust. "And one as particularly fine as Lady Anna."

"She did not deserve that, Sinclair," Gideon landed the point home.

Didn't she, though? Charles forced the stubborn thought into his head. Didn't she? For trying to talk to him. They were already bound to spend the rest of their lives together – hell, their whole lives together. They'd been forced together their entire goddamned lives. How could she ask more of him when he was already obliged to commit and be with her until he died? Why did she want more from him? Why did he need to give more? He was already giving her his *entire life.*

He put the cigar out in the crystal ash tray, watching the embers go out and the last vestiges of smoke dissipate around him.

"Anna and I will manage," Charles said instead. "I may struggle in my conversation skills with her, but I will do right by her as her husband."

Oliver scoffed derisively. "Like you just did?"

Charles met his brother's unforgiving gaze and was rather certain Oliver wanted to punch him. Actually, it looked like most of the men surrounding him wanted to do just that.

"You said you wouldn't do anything to make her unhappy or

hurt her," Oliver continued, reminding him. "I'm curious, what is it you think you just did?"

His selfishness, his self-preservation, his stubbornness, his duty, his wife. It was too much. Charles couldn't reconcile any of it. He couldn't subdue it. He didn't know what he could possibly do.

But her horrified face. Bright red with embarrassment. With shame. She'd tried to reach out to him, and in his confusion and panic, he'd slapped her away.

The guilt finally seized Charles like a cold, steel band around his chest, making it impossible to breathe. In his cowardice, his fear, he'd intentionally harmed his wife. His friends were right – it had been intentional. So that she might leave him alone. So that he could maintain the distance she'd clearly been trying to bridge. He was a coward and liar. Like the selfish bastard he was, he'd knowingly and purposely *hurt her*.

And now, he could not breathe thinking of it.

# CHAPTER 7

## ANNA

"That was horrid," Emily said in a low voice from beside Anna as they made their way to the drawing room after dinner. Genevieve and Grace were directly behind them, close enough to be part of their conversation. Amelia and Lydia, however, were a few paces ahead, muttering quietly between themselves. Anna knew it was about the dinner, and Charles and Anna.

"It was," Anna replied, her footsteps quiet on the entryway floor.

"I am sorry, Anna," Genevieve spoke in a regretful voice. "I do not understand what is plaguing Charles, but I am sorry."

Anna looked back at her future sister-in-law. "It is not for any of you to be sorry, Genevieve," Anna assured her gently. "It is done now. I kept my vow from this afternoon. Now, we may let it be."

Anna glanced at Emily as she faced forward again, finding her friend shaking her head in what seemed like disbelief or disappointment. Perhaps both.

Entering the drawing room, Lydia pulled the cord by the

fireplace to call for tea before joining everyone as they arranged themselves in the seating area before the warm fire.

"Anna," Amelia spoke as everyone settled. "Are you alright?"

"Yes," Anna said, polite but firm. "I admit to a certain level of embarrassment, but otherwise, I am unharmed."

"You needn't talk about it, Anna, if you do not wish to," Grace said in that delicately proud way she had.

Anna appreciated the words. She did not want to talk about. Her mind and heart still reeled as she tried to process what had happened this first and only time she had tried to bridge the gap between her and Charles.

A maid entered with a tea tray, which she set down on the small table before them and exited after receiving Lydia's thanks and sweet smile. Lydia leaned forward and began pouring their cups and passing them over.

Amelia picked up the conversation, noticing and respecting Anna's privacy, as well. "Next time we're all in London, it will be your Season, Grace. We'll have quite a bit of plotting to do amongst the six of us on behalf of both you and your sister." Amelia smirked as she nodded in Emily's direction before lifting her cup to her lips. Emily rolled her eyes, clearly not having changed her stance on her own situation since their afternoon tea.

Anna wasn't in a place to adequately support her friend tonight, though. Regardless of her assurances to all of them, Anna felt her thoughts and shame from the meal move to the forefront of her mind. She could not help reliving her future husband's rudeness as she tried to connect with him.

With each passing minute, Anna knew they grew closer to the gentlemen rejoining them. Her only consolation was that the night would end shortly after, but before it did, she would have to share the room with Charles again. And then, once the night was over, the next time she saw him, she would have to begin sharing a home with him for the rest of her life.

*Unless.*

Unless, she thought with dawning horror, he intended to live separately from her. She knew he'd spent much of his recent years occupying Sinclair House in London. Perhaps he planned to continue doing so, leaving her in the country at Sinclair Manor. The thought had never occurred to her before, she was shocked to realize. She had always assumed they would live together once they were married, but if he wanted nothing to do with her, which was very obviously the case, why would he?

Dread dripped down her throat, pooling in her chest as the likelihood of this possibility settled within her. Perhaps.... He did need an heir, so perhaps he would visit her enough to give her children. Anna was so eager for children, she'd always, always wanted them. She couldn't imagine not having them.

She held the teacup in her lap and wished to trace its handle to give her hands something to do as her mind replayed Charles's closed off responses and clipped tone. But she didn't. She held her cup lightly, lifting it to take a sip of the warm contents.

Of course, they would have children, her thoughts continued as she steadily held her cup and moved her eyes to whoever spoke, giving the illusion that she focused only on their conversation while her thoughts and emotions around Charles rampaged through her. Of course, they would. They had to. It was the whole purpose of this arrangement, after all. He was obligated to sire children, even if he wasn't obligated to acknowledge her or live with her. She would have children, at least. And, she consoled herself further, she would not be without family. Genevieve, Oliver, and Prudence would all be there, as would Amelia and Gideon, who lived right near Sinclair Manor, as well. Lydia and Thomas would also not be far in Coventry.

No, all would be well. She would be content, she told herself with perhaps too much conviction. She recognized how the night had her thoughts shifting from the usual disheartened acceptance of her future to a scattered panic.

"I remind you for the hundredth time today, I think we can abandon all efforts made in my regard," Emily said as Anna forced herself to focus properly on her companions. "I am destined to be a spinster, fight it as you might."

Anna noticed Lydia's brows furrowing before she looked to Genevieve, who replied to Emily's claim with surety, "We know no such thing."

"More is the delusion for you," Emily laughed into her tea.

Anna ignored her own emotions and rallied once again with the group. "We shall see, Emily."

# CHAPTER 8

## CHARLES

The men's judgment did not lessen over the course of their brandy and cigars, and Charles struggled between his stubbornness and the guilt his friends reinforced. Regardless, their combined efforts and Charles's own regret had him deciding that he should make some sort of amends with Anna tonight.

He didn't know what would come of it, good or bad or who knows what. He just knew he needed to do something because he was not this cruel and he hated, *hated*, that he hurt her. He could not leave things like that.

So, when they finally rejoined the ladies in the drawing room, his eyes went to his wife, seated on the couch next to her friend, Emily, and pointedly ignoring his entrance.

His heart pounded in his chest as he strode up to her, uncaring of their companions and the gentlemen positioning themselves throughout the warm, comfortable room.

"Would you accompany me for a turn about the room, Anna?" he asked her in a low voice that he pushed through clenched teeth. The effect wasn't quite as he intended, but perhaps that would be beneficial in ensuring his peace offering was not misunderstood as something more.

That ethereal face turned to him, schooled in a practiced indifference, but Charles noted the surprise in her light crystal eyes. She didn't say anything, just stood and took his arm.

He ignored the murmurings of the others and led her slowly around the perimeter of the room. She was quiet as they walked, but her floral scent, the heat of her body, the easy way she moved with him had his full attention. He noted her gaze on the walls, admiring the scenic paintings that tended to be mostly of the countryside.

His heart did not calm down, and neither did the contradictory and relentless emotions coursing through him. With each step they took in silence, the more potent his internal discomfort became.

This was exactly why Charles avoided her. How was he supposed to talk to her? They were an arrangement, a responsibility, but she was also his wife. The wife he hadn't chosen and didn't know if he would have chosen if he'd been given the chance. And still, there was something... else within him. Something that made him *want*.

Coventry had only been partly correct in what he said to Charles this evening. Yes, he knew how to make conversation. In fact, it was one of his strongest skills. But his lack of conversing with Anna wasn't intentional. It wasn't that he didn't know how to converse. He didn't know how to converse *with her* because of the mess of feelings she inspired in him.

He didn't know what he wanted. Charles had never been given the luxury of figuring that out. He was the eldest. He was the head of his family. He inherited his father's business. He would marry Anna.

What he did know, however, was when he was not in her company, his internal struggle lessened. She was easier to ignore.

They reached the piano, and he steered her around it and led her back to the seating area. Charles caught Oliver's eye and found his brother's gaze hard. Neither Anna or Charles had spoken at all, nor had they paused in their steady walk around the room. Charles decided it was for the best, despite their friends' collective displeasure and his own opposing thoughts. He'd remedied his cold behavior from their meal and not given any false impressions.

Anna let go of his arm and resumed her seat, and Charles moved towards his annoyed brother by the mantle. Philip and Alexander were on the other side of the fireplace, Jack stood by his youngest sister's armchair, and Gideon and Thomas stood by their wives. Charles could feel their continued judgment pressing against him as they expected him to do better by Anna.

But this was the best he could do.

"When do you leave for the country, Lord Ronan?" their hostess asked Alexander, effortlessly keeping the attention away from Charles and Anna.

"Tomorrow, Lady Coventry," Alexander answered. "The Davenports and I are traveling to Nottingham together." Charles noted Alexander glance at the youngest Davenport sibling, Grace, whose head shifted infinitesimally in the marquess's direction, as if pulled to him.

"Anna, you leave the day after next, is that right?" The Duchess of Birmingham asked his wife.

"Yes," he noticed Anna nodding out of the corner of his eye. "When do you and His Grace expect to return?"

"We depart the same day with the Sinclairs," Gideon answered. "I believe you have the same plan, Thomas?"

"You believe rightly," Thomas smiled at his brother-in-law.

"With all our imminent departures, perhaps we should end the evening?" Jack posed it as a question, but it was really a statement. He turned to where Emily and Anna sat on the sofa beside Genevieve. "Ladies?" he inquired. They both stood, as did

Grace, and Charles was struck once again by the odd irritation he'd experienced when Jack had escorted Anna into the room. Whatever other issues they had, Charles did not like someone else escorting his wife.

"We should end the evening, as well," Oliver muttered beside him as the rest of the group was saying their goodbyes, and Charles watched Anna for the last time before he saw her again for their wedding. He tilted his head towards his brother and gave a short nod, and they, too, began their farewells.

Eventually, Charles found himself before his wife.

"Charles," she said politely, her voice more aloof than it had been at dinner. "Safe travels."

Something in his chest hollowed out at the distance in her voice. It wasn't new, exactly. But it had never before seemed so severe. Or perhaps it was just his own imaginings after the events of this night and the prospect of their next meeting. Either way, it made something inside him oddly panic.

He blamed that for what happened next. His voice came out low and warm, something entirely unlike him, as he whispered, "Anna," lifting her hand and placing a kiss atop it. His skin tingled and blood heated at the feel of her soft skin against his. He waited until the surprise once again had her light blue eyes meeting his in confusion. He lifted his lips barely an inch from her hand and continued in a private voice only for her, "Until our wedding, wife."

# CHAPTER 9

## ANNA

*A*nna already had her cloaked donned as she walked slowly around her bedroom in Dunhill House. Her belongings were packed and loaded on to the waiting carriage outside, and the staff had covered the furniture in sheets until next Season. But this was the last time Anna would be in this room and it would be hers. At some point in the future, this house would belong to her son, but it would never be her home again. Starting next Season, she would live at her husband's house in London. It would be her house. Her home.

She trailed her fingers along the sheet covering the edge of her dressing table as she stepped slowly along it, feeling the cool softness against her fingertips as she reflected.

The dinner at the Coventry's two nights ago had felt... well, perhaps not a complete disaster, but hardly a success when she made her attempts to reach out to Charles. Even when he had returned to the drawing room and walked with her, she understood it as the apology he meant, as well as the reminder of the line between them when he circled the room with her on his arm and hadn't uttered a word.

Anna had never felt so low, so defeated about her upcoming

marriage as she had by the end of that night. The embarrassment at dinner, the alarming realization that he may not choose to live with her, then the reminder of the constant insurmountable distance between them. As much as she had tried to stay strong with the thoughts of her future children and surrounding family members – things that usually managed to console her – the truth was, by the end of the evening, she felt crushed in a way she couldn't recall ever feeling before. She'd always had a sense of disheartenment where her marriage was concerned, as far back as she could remember, but it had simply felt like reality. Like a sense of gloom on a rainy day. It didn't destroy you, but it dampened you. By the time came to leave Coventry House, however, after trying for the first time in her relationship, being rejected, and then forced back into the rain – it had *hurt*.

Anna's slow steps around her almost former bedroom had led her to its ornate door, and she turned around once more to observe and soak in the warmth and light floral scent of her perfume, which saturated the room.

Charles had noticed. That night, he'd seen her diminishing under the weight of her sadness and dread. And bid her farewell in the way that he did.

His voice had been so warm. Not that he had a cold voice, otherwise, but while he was always perfectly polite and tactful in all of his interactions she'd ever observed – rather like her, if she was being honest – his deep voice tended to struggle to carry warmth. She sensed he was a warm man with the way he cared for his brother, his mother, Genevieve, his friends, but he rarely showed it. Or perhaps *could* not show it.

Anna smirked as she reached for the doorknob but made no further move to leave.

That's what she was beginning to consider. Thinking on it objectively, Charles was a confident, brilliant, excessively kind, generous man with many strengths. But she wondered if perhaps softer, more tender qualities were not among them. She'd never thought on it before, more preoccupied with her own feelings where he was concerned, but with how the night had ended, that single, infinitely profound moment, Anna could not stop ruminating on the fact that there may be more to Charles and his feelings towards this marriage than she had originally thought.

She was not foolish or some blind, young girl in love. Of course, she knew he wanted to maintain the distance between them. But perhaps... perhaps there was a part of him, the part that spoke with warmth and called her 'wife,' that could want something different from their relationship. She could be wrong, of course. Again, she had never been a particularly foolish person, but when faced with the inevitable, unchangeable future, she would choose hope and happiness over defeat and sadness whenever she could.

And so, she did. Anna chose to be happy, to build a happy future for herself. Herself and Charles. To the fullest extent that she could.

Dispelling a contented sigh, Anna turned, opening the door and stepping through it. She walked down the hall towards the stairs, tables all lifeless and empty of their usual flowers and also covered in white sheets.

When she left the vortex of her dejection, she could see how Charles had shown her a few times this Season that he had more than just a desire for distance between them. The way he'd called her beautiful and danced with her more than once. The way he'd looked at her at Oliver and Genevieve's wedding. The kiss on her hand. The warmth of his voice. The way he called her 'wife,' acknowledging their upcoming wedding with what sounded like anticipation rather than dread.

All of those moments this Season... those were all firsts. Never before had he done any of those things. Anna did not know what exactly it meant or what he alternatively desired.

But now that she'd thought and thought about it without the prejudice of her own feelings swaying her, she would wager some part of him wanted something different between them. Not only that, she was curious if Charles realized this, himself.

There was a slight bounce to her steps as Anna descended the stairs, her hand trailing along the intricate wooden banister as she went. It was new, she knew, as she reached the landing and walked with hope in her steps past the entryway table towards the large, elegantly carved front door. And the desire was small if it was there. A kernel within Charles's fortified and established stubbornness. But it *could be*.

She smiled to herself, closing the front door behind her and taking the stone steps to where her parents stood with the servants readying the carriages for their journey ahead, back to their country home.

Because if that desire *was* there, it could also *grow*.

And she was his wife. It was her job to help and support her husband. She would. In all things, she would. Including this one.

This time, she made a vow to herself, one she did not intend to share with her friends or family. Stepping into the carriage and moving towards the far seat by the window, she sat and gazed out of it as she waited for her parents to join her and their journey to begin.

She would water that desire of her husband's, and she would keep reaching out to him until that line between them was finally destroyed. Until all that remained was the warmth that had spread through her when his lips met her skin.

# CHAPTER 10

## CHARLES

"*D*o you plan on hiding out here forever?" Oliver's voice pulled Charles's head up towards the door of Sinclair Manor's study.

"I am not hiding out here," Charles replied steadfastly as Oliver walked directly to the corner side table to Charles's right, where he sat at his desk poring over last month's ledger.

Filling a tumbler, Oliver scoffed. "You're an awful liar," he said, holding up the bottle in Charles's direction in question. The light from the window reflected off the crystal decanter, casting a rainbow of colors on the single bookshelf built into the dark green wall behind the small table.

Charles picked up his own near empty tumbler and held it out to his brother. Oliver stepped over and took the crystal glass to refill it before handing it back and returning the decanter to its place.

Charles leaned back in his chair, angling towards the room's two large windows before which his brother stood. The fire crackled in the fireplace behind the desk, filling the room with warmth.

"I am not lying. These accounts cannot review themselves."

Oliver arched a brow at him before walking around to the front of the desk and dropping into the dark green velvet sofa, which was situated behind a set of cushioned chairs and perfectly matched the room's wallpaper. Charles followed the movement from his seat, continuing to face him.

"You know Mother will come and find you eventually," Oliver reminded him, ignoring Charles's claim.

"She is welcome to," Charles said coolly, taking a sip of his brandy.

"And is she also welcome to pull you into the wedding preparations happening throughout the Manor, from which you are *not* hiding?" Oliver pushed. He relaxed annoyingly in the corner of the sofa, one arm draped along its back, while the other held his glass against the armrest, his ankle crossed over his knee.

He really was a prat.

Charles straightened his posture, taking another swig before placing his tumbler on his desktop once again. "If anything requires my attention or input, I will, of course, provide it."

Oliver shook his head, clearly not believing him.

Charles didn't need to, nor would he, tell Oliver how precise his original claim had been. Of course, he was hiding. Yes, he would give input if required of him, but he intended to stay safely locked away from the commotion taking place throughout his home. He didn't want to see it. He didn't want to participate or be involved. He wanted to sit in his study and lose himself in his work and forget that in a matter of a few very short weeks, practically days, he would be a married man.

"There's no point in my asking, but I'll do so anyway," Oliver broke into his thoughts. "Have you heard from Anna at all?"

"Not calling her Lady Anna anymore?" Charles muttered,

deflecting as he bent his head over the sheet of numbers that now seemed like a jumble when a few minutes before, they had made complete sense.

"She will be my sister soon after all," Oliver said obnoxiously, albeit accurately. "Have you heard from her?" he repeated, his voice shifting closer to that hard tone he'd been using more frequently these past months when Charles was behaving disappointingly with regard to his own wife.

"Why should I hear from her?" Charles replied, his voice low.

"As much as you claimed I was a fool with Genevieve, I very much doubt there is a greater one in existence than you, Charles."

"She will be here in a matter of days," Charles said, pretending that he understood the mess of ink he kept his eyes determinedly fixed to. "We can –."

"Talk then?" Oliver finished for him in a sarcastically helpful voice. "Of course, you can. As you've always been so excessively loquacious with your betrothed."

Charles lifted his eyes to stare at his brother, the warning in them clear to tread carefully.

"Concern yourself with your own wife, Oliver," Charles's voice was hard as ice.

"My wife is concerned for you, too," Oliver countered. "And her *friend*."

"Your wife is expecting and in the process of shifting residences," Charles bent his head toward the page of accounts again, reaching for his tumbler with one hand. "Perhaps you both should concern yourselves with that."

Oliver and Genevieve were moving to the nearby Boncroft Hall now that Charles's wedding was upon them. He'd tried to get them to stay, wanting their presence more for his own sake than anyone else's, but they had insisted.

He noticed Oliver stand in his periphery but didn't lift his gaze as his brother tossed back his liquor and made his way back to the side table to return the glass.

"Anna deserves a husband, Charles," Oliver's voice was low and oddly gentle compared to the overall tone of their conversation thus far. "You are the only one who can give that to her. Don't be a fool."

And with that, his brother crossed the room and left Charles alone in the study.

He let out a breath before drinking down half his remaining brandy in a single gulp. Without permission, his mind went back, yet again, to the last time he saw Anna. That evening in the Coventry House drawing room. He had recalled the feel of her skin against his lips many times since that night months ago. The way her eyes had watched him in shock, her unusual mouth parted slightly. He'd never kissed any part of her before, and his lips still tingled every time the memory relived itself in his mind. He was still shocked by the awareness that heated its way through him that night, the one simple and yet wildly complicated moment.

Oliver was right. Of course, Anna deserved a husband. And no one else *could* ever give that to her. There had only ever been one husband for her. *Him*. Whether either one of them liked it or not.

But he wasn't sure if he was capable of giving it to her.

# CHAPTER 11

## ANNA

*T*he carriage rolled to a stop, jostling Anna one last time. She was exhausted from traveling, but they were finally here. Sinclair Manor. Her new home.

"We have arrived," her father announced unnecessarily from the bench opposite her and her mother as he peered out of the window.

"Yes," her mother replied tiredly.

It was another moment before a footman opened the door to let them out. Anna followed her mother into the cold November air, and her eyes went of their own accord to the large Manor before her. She'd been here several times over the years, but she had never looked at it with the eyes of a resident. It was exactly how she remembered, grand and beautiful. In a week, not only would this be her home, but she would be the Lady of this impressive Manor.

Standing in front of it, waiting to receive her, was her new family and the whole of her new household. Charles and

Prudence stood in front, the latter's smile completely uncontained. Close behind them stood Oliver and Genevieve, also watching their party with warmth and welcome.

She knew Oliver and Genevieve were in the process of moving to their new home close by; Genevieve had written to her about it. Prudence would be accompanying them at least until the birth of the baby. Anna was glad they were here now, though. She would much rather everyone stayed at Sinclair Manor, but understood both newlywed couples would need their own space. Anna was still somewhat unsure if she wanted it, but they were so close, she reassured herself she'd never feel the loss of their company long.

Her eyes traced down the stone arches and carvings of her new home until they found him. Her heart started to beat a little faster. Charles stood stoic as ever, handsome, immovable, breathtaking. His blonde hair was bright in the sunlight, his fair cheeks flushed from the near winter cold. He didn't smile, giving off no warmth, and yet she heard that low voice in her head once more.

*Until our wedding, wife.*

Somewhere within that unsmiling man could be a real husband for Anna, she was sure of it. It was based off four words, instinct, and wishful thinking, and of course, she knew how nonsensical that was, but when the future was set, she much preferred to walk to it with a sense of hope. She'd spent the past months since the end of last Season purposefully and determinedly building that hope up and reinforcing it.

Even now, with this new lens securely in place, she thought she could identify traces of the deeply hidden desire within him. It was in the way his unearthly pale blue eyes fixed on hers, not looking away. It was so rare for him to look at her so directly and for solid moments of time.

She took it as yet another positive sign. There was hope. They could be happy. They *would* be happy.

Because Charles Sinclair was everything Anna wanted in man, in a husband, in the person who was the other half of her life. She'd known that for some time. Her friends and family thought she didn't, that because she stayed on her side of the divide between them, she didn't want Charles. But even from her side of the fence, she'd watched him when no one else was looking. When he wasn't aware either. It was more than just his beauty. So, so much more. He was confident, wise, strong. He took his time. Was always cool and calm, the voice of reason. And he was terribly, deeply loving.

Charles was a man she could rely on and trust to stand beside her through life. If not for the distance he enforced between them, she would have leaned into that knowledge a long time ago. Instead, she'd spent the past years not giving into her desire for him as a companion, partner, husband.

In truth, as she thought on it the past months, that night at Coventry House had been doomed to fail from the start. She did not know Charles well, but she *understood* him. And with the benefit of hindsight and honest reflection, she realized she should have reached out to him more privately rather than in front of their friends. Anna and Charles were much the same in many ways, and if their roles had been reversed that night, she might have had trouble navigating a new dynamic after eighteen years, made all the more difficult with an audience. She would have preferred him reaching out to her more quietly, perhaps during a peaceful walk, just the two of them.

"Come, dear," Anna's father whispered gently to her, breaking into her reverie as she and Charles drank each other in with their eyes. Anna kept her head high and followed her parents to greet their welcoming party.

"Welcome, Lord Dunhill, Lady Dunhill," Prudence practically sang. "And *finally*, my new daughter." Her usual exaggerated, playful tone could not hide the genuine note of wonder beneath it, and Anna turned to find her mother-in-law's eyes glassy. "Welcome home," she finished.

"Thank you," Anna replied with a small smile, and her eyes looked up of their own accord to Charles's face. Her parents continued greeting Prudence and the others, the servants of both households began busying themselves unpacking their belongings, but it all happened in another world.

There was only Anna and Charles. His light blue eyes, so like his mother's in shape and color, yet so completely different in how they expressed themselves. She couldn't tell anything of what he thought, and her own face remained tactfully schooled in indifference. But those eyes were on hers. And she had come home. To him.

# CHAPTER 12

## CHARLES

*S*omething was different. He wasn't sure if it was him or if it was her – or both – but something, *everything* was different. Charles's heart had yet to stop racing. Since the moment Anna stepped out of that carriage and looked up at the Manor, his heart had been making every concerted effort to break free of his chest.

She was a vision. Had she always been? Wrapped in a heavy cloak, her red hair glittering in the winter sun, looking up at the Manor. Of course, Anna had been here before. Many, many times over the years, but never once had she looked at his home like... like it was hers.

Then, those crystal eyes found him and held his gaze.

What's more, he held hers.

The activity bustled around them as they stayed locked onto each other.

"Anna," he finally spoke, his voice cool and polite, matching his expression. "Welcome."

"Thank you, Charles," she replied softly, something unfamiliar sparkling in her eyes that made him both nervous and something else he could not place.

Oliver and Genevieve stepped forward in his periphery, taking that as their cue. He watched as their happy expressions had Anna's striking lips pulling up.

"Genevieve," his wife quietly exclaimed as she noticed how much his future niece or nephew had grown these past months. "You are *glowing*, my friend."

Genevieve rested a hand atop her stomach. "He or she has come along quite a bit, haven't they?" She eyed her stomach sweetly before looking at Anna again. "And it's *sister*, now."

Charles watched, his chest clenching as Anna took Genevieve's free hand and kissed her knuckles. "Sister and friend," she replied, holding their clasped hands to her heart.

"If you two are quite through being emotional," Oliver interrupted, for which Charles was grateful, as his own emotions were becoming increasingly difficult. "I do believe everyone is waiting for us."

He was right, of course. Their parents had all gone inside, as had much of the staff. All those that remained were busy gathering the remainder of the Lucases belongings.

"Oliver, there is not a soul alive that would consider you anything but the most emotional of the four of us," Genevieve countered accurately, pulling her hand from Anna's to wrap it around her husband's arm. His sister-in-law winked at his wife before letting Oliver guide her towards the house.

"You match me rather well, my gem, do not try to pretend otherwise," Charles heard Oliver respond as they walked away.

Soon, it was just him and Anna left outside, and he had yet to take his eyes from her. He still couldn't get his heart to settle. The way she smiled at Genevieve, the happiness bursting from her as she greeted his family. *Their* family.

His wife was warmth and joy and love, and she no longer diminished it in his presence. Even more surprising, though, was the new, resulting feeling within himself at witnessing it. Charles wanted to soak it all into his own soul, basking in it to soothe and calm his heart. As if this, *she*, was the solution to the very tempests she caused within him.

Anna faced him again, her gaze resting on his with an openness he could never before recall seeing. The loveliness of those eyes, that expression was not lost on him. She looked beautiful. Surreal and breathtaking, and he could not take it.

Charles silently held out his arm, and once she'd taken it, he led his wife into her home. Another thing he'd done many times in the past, but never before had it meant so much.

Because this time, Anna would not leave. This time, it was finally hers.

Stopping in the entryway, he helped her out of her cloak and gloves, revealing the green dress she wore underneath. Her soft floral scent assaulted his senses, and he breathed her in, another knot of tension he hadn't registered easing in his chest. His gaze lingered along the column of her neck and shoulders, and he was struck with an entirely new and unwelcome urge to trace the pale, freckled skin with his fingertips.

Shaking off the desire, he offered his arm to her again and began to lead her towards the drawing room where the others waited. As they crossed the entryway, he heard Anna's small intake of breath. In fact, if it hadn't been so quiet around them, he might have missed it altogether, but he would not have missed how her feet stopped moving. He peered at her out of the corner of his eye to see her gaze roaming over the decorations with which his mother had covered their white halls over the past two weeks. The extra tables, the especially ornate candelabras, the unreasonable number of hellebores artfully displayed in their most expensive vases.

"Mother has had quite a bit of time to plan how she wanted the wedding to look," he found himself offering by way of explanation.

Anna turned to him, her large eyes blinking once.

It wasn't often, if ever, that either of them volunteered

conversation, and he wasn't sure what prompted him to do so now.

She faced the room again, keeping her expression neutral as she replied, surprising him just as much as his own words had, "Eighteen years, to be precise." She paused before adding, "It looks lovely."

"I am sure if there are any adjustments you would like made, Mother would be all too happy to embrace them. We still have a week."

He didn't know how he was conversing with her, or she with him, so... so *easily*, but somehow, they were. What precisely changed between them, and why was it so effective? Never before had they successfully broken their usual protocol.

Charles pondered it as he continued to watch her, unable to resist, his heart a heavy beat behind his ribs. Perhaps now that their marriage was finally upon them after years of avoiding it, avoiding each other, their respective defeat allowed them to face what was no longer avoidable.

Perhaps there was something freeing about defeat.

Or possibly, probably, it was Anna. The difference he sensed in her naturally pulling something different from him without his consent.

Regardless, the part of him that loved the sound of her sweet voice felt strong as she answered, the two of them still unmoving in the entryway, "No, it is all quite beautiful as it is."

"Are you certain?" he asked without conscious thought, his mind too absorbed in watching her unique, mind-altering lips move as she spoke. "Do you not have a favorite flower or food you'd like at your own wedding?"

Ah, there it was. Of course, the usual riot of his emotions would not allow him to continue enjoying this conversation with his wife for long. Guilt pierced his chest with the sharpness of a rapier. Eighteen years and he did not know Anna's favorite flower or food.

She must have realized this, too, as she peered up at him, her crystal eyes shining with bitter amusement.

"My favorite flower is not in bloom this time of year," she informed him. "And your mother has already included trifle in the menu in addition to our wedding cake. We settled the menu before we left London this past Season."

Of course. His wife had a sweet tooth. He did know she enjoyed desserts, finishing them in their entirety at every meal, but he hadn't known they were her favorite. The knowledge had the very corners of his lips pulling up in spite of the burgeoning return of his turmoil. He didn't miss how her eyes zeroed in on the action.

"Well, then," he replied, his voice back to its usual cool timbre. But he had to ask, "What is your favorite flower?"

Her eyes lifted to his again, her gaze penetrating and shining brighter. She stared at him for an endless minute, and he could not look away. Charles didn't understand the reason behind her heavy inspection, but he hooked into her eyes just as much as she did his.

Never looking away, her expression blank but eyes unrelenting, she answered.

"Recently, I have found myself rather taken with foxgloves."

His heart, which had calmed over the course of their bizarrely easy conversation, tried to break his ribs with renewed vigor.

He saw her again, red hair pinned with pearls, pale blue dress matching the sky and his own eyes, radiant and beautiful, walking down the aisle where he stood waiting. Foxgloves held in her steady, gloved hands. Those crystal blue eyes in the shape of perfect almonds fastened to him and only him.

Like now.

"Is that so? May I ask how recently?" he asked in a low voice. That same low, warm voice that had left him instinctively when he bid his wife farewell in London.

"Since Genevieve and Oliver's wedding," she said, confirming his suspicion, her voice also quiet.

He needed to hear it. He didn't know why, but damn it, he needed to hear it.

"Why?" Charles pushed, nerves clutching at the thought. He also didn't know if it was in anticipation of her confirmation or denial, or which he would prefer to hear.

Blue eyes never wavered from blue.

"Since you stood at the altar with your brother," she whispered. "Watching me walk towards you as if you had never beheld anything more beautiful, more wondrous in your entire life."

And he never had.

# CHAPTER 13

## ANNA

*This* was what she should have done all those months ago. A quiet, intimate conversation, just the two of them, no spectators or bystanders. No past or preconceptions. Just them. Just the moment.

Her reflection had been right during their time apart – she had done them a disservice when she attempted to connect with him with an audience, even one made up of their closest friends. They were so similar, Anna and Charles, they were both cognizant and well-versed in how to appropriately behave in front of others. And building a bridge between them was a deeply personal act for people such as them. Even more so when considered with the polite, weighted distance that had settled between them over practically their entire lives.

They were finally speaking to each other. Not with obligations and expectations crushing them. Oddly, it felt like now that the weight of their past and anticipation of their future lifted, it also made things between them easier. Granted, they'd been in each other's company for less than thirty minutes, but these thirty minutes had been more strikingly different from any other time they'd spent together.

Charles and Anna still stood in the lavishly decorated entry hall, her arm wrapped around his, their eyes unwavering from one another. She hadn't expected to be so honest with him, to show him how much that moment in the church during Oliver and Genevieve's wedding had meant to her, how much *he* meant to her. But he had asked. And she would never lie to him.

She waited, heart in her throat, as she refused to be the first to speak after her admission.

The moment broke before Charles could form a response by the clicking of shoes on a wooden floor walking hastily before coming to an abrupt halt. They both turned towards the sound to see Prudence standing in the doorway to the drawing room, her thin lips slightly parted and light blue eyes wide as she took in the two of them at a standstill by the large center table of the entry hall.

But Prudence was nothing if not quick on her feet. Once she registered their attention on her, she closed her mouth and blinked away her shock, replacing it swiftly with her usual smile. As if spotting Anna and Charles actively taking some time alone together was the most normal occurrence in the world.

"There you are, dears," she said in a voice that *almost* pulled off nonchalance.

"We are coming through, Mother," Charles spoke. "Anna was just admiring your decorations."

"Nonsense," Prudence replied too loudly. She paused for the briefest of moments to regulate herself, it seemed, and proceeded with more delicacy. That she very obviously assessed and schemed in her mind was not lost on Anna, likely nor on Charles. "I only came to ask you to take Anna up to her room. She has not seen it before, and I haven't the time. I'm sure you understand, Anna." She smiled apologetically at Anna, the glint in her eye obvious clear across the hall, before she turned back to her son, speaking hurriedly and not giving him a chance to reply. "Won't you, dear? Thank you, and do not hurry back."

Prudence practically tossed the last words over her shoulder as she rushed back into the drawing room, shutting the large, white and gold trimmed door behind her. Clearly, they were no longer welcome at tea.

A beat of silence passed as they both caught up to the speed with which Prudence acted.

"Well," Charles's deep voice finally spoke, dropping his arm and her hand with it.

"She's quite subtle," Anna offered, her head tilted ever so slightly as she stared at the door in her mother-in-law's wake.

"As a drum," he muttered.

Anna's head shot to him in surprise, a smile pulling at her lips. Not her usual small, polite one, but a proper smile as she took in Charles's face. He looked taken aback by his words to her, as well, if the way he glanced at her was any indication. But he seemed to notice the bright, disbelieving eyes with which she watched him before she laughed.

She lifted her hand to her chest, feeling like the happiness would somehow burst free if she did not hold it in, and she gave her husband a full mouth, white toothed grin in exchange for the first joke he'd ever given her.

"Indeed," she agreed, unable to stop smiling as she traced the sharp angles of Charles's face with her eyes, feeling like she both knew this face as well as her own and had never seen it before. And he seemed to be cataloguing her, too.

She dropped her hand and dimmed her smile, unable to compose it completely, as she shifted the moment. "I will not be staying in my usual rooms?" she asked.

Anna's parents always stayed in the west wing of the Manor when they visited, and she had occupied the same rooms next to them for as long as she remembered coming here.

Charles cleared his throat. "No," he said and turned towards the wide staircase, rounding the table as he approached it.

She followed beside him, their steps quiet on the luxuriously thick rug beneath their feet. Placing her hand delicately on the light chocolate brown banister with the same detailed carvings that decorated the rest of the house, she trailed her fingers along the smooth wood as they made their way upstairs.

"Why not?" she asked when Charles did not continue.

"You are the Lady of the Manor now," his voice had abandoned that elusive warm tone she'd now heard twice and gone back to its usual cool composure. Anna found she did not mind. She had started to understand this was who Charles was, and she should not only admire him but *accept* him.

He continued, "Or at least you will be in a week. Those are your rooms now."

Anna's breath caught when she understood his words. "Your wife's rooms."

Of course. Of course, she'd have the Lady of the Manor's rooms now. She hadn't even considered it, but of course. She'd been so used to their usual routine, her usual rooms during her usual visit, she had completely forgotten her old rooms had been only temporary.

They reached the landing and turned to walk down the yellow and cream patterned hall. Charles glanced sidelong at her, confirming, "Yes."

"They are beside yours?" she asked the obvious, unsure if excitement or nerves made her voice breathless and heart pitter patter in her chest.

"Yes," he answered simply, facing forward, his stride long and oddly affecting her with its masculinity. That, coupled with the wood pine scent in the air between them and what her new rooms meant.... Anna tried not to show how her breathing changed, her body feeling warm and soft in an unknown, but not unpleasant way.

They walked silently down the hallway before stopping at another large, lavishly carved door. Charles turned the ornate gold doorknob and stepped to the side to let her proceed to the center of her new room undeterred.

It was larger than any room she'd ever had, even larger than the one she usually occupied at Sinclair Manor. The walls were patterned in a soft, periwinkle blue with birds sitting atop cream colored branches. The large drapes on the window were open, letting in the last of the day's wintery sunlight. The large four poster bed looked extravagant and inviting with its gold sheets and sheer curtains tied artfully open. The armoire, mirror, and dressing table and chair were carved in a light wood with the finest detailing Anna had ever seen. The fireplace was lit with two cream armchairs and a small table angled before it. And still there was so much room to spare.

The Lady of the Manor's room.

She was gawking, she knew, as she took it all in.

The happiness from the success of her new perspective, the wonderful interactions with Charles, the meaning and beauty of her new rooms, all combined and overflowed within her. So much so, she felt she may burst, her body unable to contain the joy of the past half hour alone.

Anna turned around to see Charles standing in the open doorway, his gaze once again watching her every reaction while she hadn't been looking.

"It's beautiful, Charles," she told him truthfully, spinning around on the spot slowly so she could take it all in again. "I've never been in rooms as lovely as these."

"You can change anything you want. They're yours to do with as you please. As is the whole Manor," Charles said, his voice once again soft.

She made her way full circle again to face him. "Thank you," she said sincerely. Charles may have trouble expressing what he felt in words, but he did express it in other ways, she realized.

Now that she paid attention and did not wallow in self-pity as she had for eighteen years, she could recognize the moments clearly. That was twice already since her arrival that he tried to make their home into what she wanted. He wanted her to be comfortable. He wanted her to make his home hers.

He nodded, looking over her shoulder to something behind her. But Anna didn't pay attention to that. Instead, she tried to calm her now galloping heart that pounded a wild beat as the most insane, likely very stupid, thought entered her mind.

Today was so different. It was so marvelous. Charles was marvelous.

It was stupid. She knew it was stupid. She was mostly absolutely certain that it would probably shatter whatever was happening today. The fragile ease and connection between them. But the day, the moment was too perfect, too joyful, not to be a little stupid.

She needed to do it. As much as she needed her next breath, she needed this.

Before she lost her nerve, Anna took slow, measured steps towards him, and he shifted his gaze back to hers, warily watching her approach. She held his stunning, light blue eyes the color of the sky on its clearest day. His gaze was shuttered, likely surprised and wondering what she meant to do, or trying to decipher whatever expression she wore. Happiness, fear, bravery, nerves, delight, reluctance, eagerness, need. All of it.

She stepped closer to him than she'd ever been, even while dancing. His baby blue eyes never left hers. Her heartbeat never calmed. She lifted a hand and gently placed it on his chest, feeling the jittery joy compound within her when she felt the matching rapid beat of his own heart. He wasn't unaffected at all. She knew he wasn't, but it thrilled and pleased her, making her braver, to feel the proof.

Lifting up on her toes, she reached her other hand up behind his neck and pulled his face towards hers as she closed her eyes and pressed her lips against his. She'd never kissed him before. She'd never kissed *anyone* before, obviously. There had only ever been Charles in Anna's life. And she wasn't sure what to do next as she waited for him to respond.

She hoped he could feel the same heat she did when their lips touched. She didn't know if his eyes were open and watching her, unwilling to open her own to check.

A beat passed.

Then, another.

Anna began to feel the creeping edge of foolishness break through whatever insanity possessed her.

But then, Charles's arms encircled her waist like a vise, wrapping around her small frame so fully, she felt immediately surrounded by him in the most exquisite way. He pulled her body completely to his, erasing even the idea of space between them, and tilted his head as he finally kissed her back with such tenderness, she thought her heart may break from it.

And if she thought she felt heated before, she realized now she hadn't known the meaning of the word.

Anna's blood ignited, an inferno coming to life within her, in her very blood.

He unwrapped one of his long arms and lifted it to cup her cheek with his hand. Her lips parted slightly as a soft moan left her without permission at the indescribable sweetness of the action.

Charles took the opening and dipped his tongue into her mouth, stroking hers. She gasped at the sensation, feeling something within her melt and start to gather in her core. She felt her body softening for him even as she tentatively matched the movements of his tongue with her own, heat coursing through her.

The kiss was slow, deep, and the sweetest thing she had ever experienced.

Charles's heart continued to beat faster and faster beneath

her palm, mirroring her own. She could feel the hardness of his body's reaction through the layers of fabric between them. An instinct bloomed within her, an intuitive desire to move against him, but she withheld, losing herself in the most amazing kiss possible.

The hand on her cheek moved gently into her hair and urged her tenderly to angle her head a bit more as he deepened the kiss.

Another soft, sweet moan moved through her and escaped from her mouth into his.

At once, the spell broke at the sound.

Charles wrenched himself away from Anna's arms, unraveling his own from around her, as if he'd been burned. He was a foot away from her, framed in the doorway, before she could even register what happened.

His lips were parted, his breaths leaving him in pants, as he stared at her wide-eyed. She could guess she looked exactly the same.

They studied one another before Charles muttered a low, "Excuse me," and practically ran from the room.

Anna stood frozen for a moment before her fingers reached up and touched her bottom lip. Turning around, she walked back into her new room towards the full-length mirror, stopping before it.

She looked the same. Slightly travel worn. Hair in need of a bit of care. But her face was flushed. Her chest moving rapidly as her heart still struggled to settle.

Anna met her own eyes in the mirror, unsure if she'd set them back with her uncontrollable impulsivity on the day they had finally taken a baby step forward. But as she moved her hand to her excessively freckled cheek, the taste of Charles still on her tongue, Anna knew she'd do anything necessary to bring them together. To truly, honestly have her husband be hers in every sense of the word.

# CHAPTER 14

## CHARLES

*C*harles hurried out of Anna's room, the taste of her still on his lips spurring his exit. He didn't seek his closest sanctuary, his bedroom, which was still too close to her. Instead, he tore through the hallway, launching himself down the stairs, and straight to his study. The dark walls embraced him in their comfort as soon as he entered and shut the door.

He crossed the room with the same quick strides to the far corner. Charles poured himself a generous glass of brandy from the side table and immediately gulped it down. He hoped the burn of the liquor would rid the sweet, honey taste of her from his lips.

It didn't.

Charles put the glass down, bracing his hands on either side of the table, and dropped his head, still trying to regulate his breathing.

She had kissed him. Never once, *never once*, had they kissed.

And it was amazing.

That kiss was perfect. Gentle and sweet, calm and sure, unexpected and unassuming in its fire. Its heat was measured, deep, and all-encompassing. He could still feel it crawling along his skin, pumping with his blood inside his veins. His body was still lost to it. His lips tingled with the memory of hers against them. His fingers itched to be on her skin, in her hair. His cock, the treacherous thing, strained against the confines of his clothing.

He took a deep breath and straightened, grabbing the decanter once more to pour another drink. Stoppering the bottle, he picked up his glass and stepped the few feet to his desk chair and fell into it, slouching down and facing the windows. His eyes fixed to the darkening sky outside as he lifted the glass to his mouth once more, now knowing it wouldn't wash away her taste. As his heart rate calmed, he knew her taste would be ingrained in him forever. And a significant part of him was beyond joyful of the fact.

Anna had kissed him. Their first kiss. *His* first kiss, and he knew hers, too. And the beauty of it shattered his entire mind, his thread of composure. It was the best moment of his life, he realized, and that concerned him greatly. How could he ever resist her if he wanted her?

The crystal stayed cupped between his palms as he continued to gaze unseeingly into the darkening room. He'd kissed her back. How could he not? He had been shocked when she stepped up to him and placed her lips against his. The feel of her hand resting lightly on his chest, touching him like she never had before. The softness of those unbelievable lips on him. Her sanity stealing floral scent stronger and closer than ever before.

His entire world had stopped in that moment. He forgot how to think, how to breathe, how to do anything.

He *had* to kiss her back. It felt like nothing else in the world mattered, nor could ever matter, except kissing her. Nothing else existed except Anna and her lips. And he had to kiss her.

He drank half the liquor in his glass. His nerves slowly began to calm, and he grasped things more effectively. Like the greatest trouble of it, which was not that he'd enjoyed it, loved it, wanted to experience it again and again for the rest of his life. No, what concerned him most was how the kiss had felt like *them*. Like Anna. Like him.

He tossed back the last of his drink and leaned forward in his chair. The cold room was fully dark now, and he didn't bother lighting any candles as he leaned his elbows on his desk and dropped his head into his hands. He had to get up and join the others in the drawing room. Join them for dinner. Spend time with their families. Spend time with Anna.

If Charles had thought his emotions were tumultuous before, they were goddamn world-ending today. He groaned at his own melodrama, which was usually unlike him.

It had felt so easy to talk to her. It was *never* easy to talk to her, and yet today, they spoke to each other. Like they were in it together. For the first time in their literal lives, they connected. And he didn't know what to do about it. If he even wanted it. Or if it was a massive betrayal to himself to want it. To want *her*. The woman he was forced to marry.

He'd been confused before, but the feelings he could feel coursing through him after today…. Talking to her. Kissing her. They were more than he could have expected. His mind, heart, and body all felt like a mess of contradictions, and he couldn't see the way out.

The door opened, breaking into Charles's thoughts, and he lifted his head to see the outline of his brother in the dark doorway.

"What are you doing?" Oliver asked, stepping into the room. "Why are you sitting in the dark?"

"Anna kissed me," Charles said without any semblance of his usual tact.

"*Did* she now?" Charles didn't need to see to know his younger brother had a ridiculous grin on his face. "About damn time one of you did something. Wait a moment." Oliver left the room and came back with a candle from the hall. Using it to light the candles around the room, he asked, "So, what happened?"

"I told you already," Charles stood from his desk and went to refill his tumbler and pour a drink for his brother. "She kissed me. And I am already regretting sharing that with you."

Oliver took a seat on the sofa as Charles joined him, handing him his glass. "It's the first time you've ever shared anything like this with me, so I am certain we are long overdue."

"You're a gossip," Charles stated matter-of-factly.

"Hardly," Oliver still had a smile painted on his obnoxious face, but his eyes were sincere as he looked at his brother. "In truth, Charles, this is a good thing. How do you feel?"

Charles rubbed a hand down his face again as he reclined on the couch, then pushed it through his hair. He revealed more than he normally would again – he blamed the singularity of the day for his candid answers. "Conflicted."

"Why?" The smile finally left Oliver's face as his brows pulled down.

How to explain? He struggled with what Anna represented. His choice of love and life robbed from him when he was nothing but a child. And yet, she was very likely everything he could imagine wanting in a woman. But a part of him, the bitter part, didn't know if that was because she was all he was ever *allowed* to want. Either way, though, it was clear from today, from that kiss, that he did want her. He didn't want to want her, but he did. And that was yet another thing he could not control.

Charles could not explain all of this. Not in a way that made sense. Not in a way that didn't make him sound absolutely mad, which he was sure was exactly what these opposing feelings and desires were. Madness. He crossed his ankle over his knee and sipped the amber liquor in his glass, unable to answer.

"Did you kiss her back, at least?" Oliver asked, moving on from the previous question.

"I did." His mind went back to the feel of her in his arms, how well she fit against him like he knew she would. He could hold her small frame entirely within the confines of his arms, and it made him feel so *whole* with her in them so completely.

"Thank heavens for small miracles," Oliver sighed dramatically. Then, he scoffed, "Perhaps that was the trick of it then. All the times we all tried to shove you both together, perhaps we should have just left you alone. You and Anna are both oddly similar and rather independent. It's good we'll be leaving for Boncroft by your wedding day. Privacy seems best."

Charles tapped his fingers against the glass in his hand. Of course, Anna and he bore many similarities. Charles would even wager there was no one more alike to him than her, just from what he observed of her over the years, how she spoke, how she behaved. But he could not adequately assess the truth in the rest of Oliver's suggestions. Is that why things were different today? Easier? Making such... *progress*, whether he wanted it or not?

They sat in companionable silence for a bit, finishing their drinks, until Charles stood. "We should prepare for dinner." He returned his glass to the side table before turning for the door. Oliver had also stood and followed him, and before Charles could pass him for the exit, his brother blocked his path.

Oliver's face was sober and his voice low when he spoke, "I know you're conflicted and have been for some time. I do not pretend to understand it. But today was a good step for you both. Follow it, and don't be a fool."

Charles took a full breath, inhaling and exhaling through his nose. He nodded, then continued towards the door.

He didn't know if he could do as Oliver advised. Even if he did want nothing more than to kiss Anna again.

# CHAPTER 15

## ANNA

"It really is beautiful," Anna's mother said, a hand against her own cheek as her glassy eyes trailed the dress Anna wore. They gathered in her new rooms, Anna, her mother, Charles's mother, and Genevieve; the ladies surrounding her as they admired the final product of her wedding gown.

"Truly lovely," Anna agreed, spinning around from facing the ladies to inspect her reflection in the mirror. "I cannot believe what you've accomplished, Mother," she told Prudence honestly.

Prudence had brought the dress to Sinclair Manor from London, and she must have worked on it nonstop since because the simple, elegantly fitted, crisp white dress had transformed into an absolute work of art. Detailed embroidery covered the dress. Prudence had hand-stitched vines and vines of flowers and leaves from the edge of her long sleeves to her shoulders, along the neckline and bodice with the addition of pearls, and straight down to the hem. It must have taken countless hours of painstaking work. The shade of the thread Prudence used was just slightly more cream than the gleaming white of the dress, and it made the intricate artwork of flowers and leaves pop slightly against the silk. The result was extravagant and breathtaking, and Anna had never felt more beautiful. Somehow, the white silk, the unbreaking floral patterns, the perfect fit suited everything about her. Both her taste and her features. In this, she *felt* like the Lady of Sinclair Manor.

"I can do many a thing when I set my mind to it," Prudence winked.

Anna laughed lightly, turning around to face her mother-in-law. "Of that, I have no doubt," she met those eyes that were her favorite color in all the world.

"Is that so?" she replied. "I would think if anyone were to doubt it, it would be you, given the unreasonably headstrong son I was unable to outsmart these eighteen years and that I am now handing to you." She spoke with a smile, but Anna could sense the true regret beneath her words.

"You outsmarted Oliver countless times," Genevieve offered in her sweet voice by way of comfort.

Prudence scoffed, waving a hand in the air. "As if that presented any difficult," she said. "Oliver is a sweet boy. He has always been led by his heart. Charles, on the other hand, is through and through his father. Both brilliant, both self-possessed, both stubborn as mules and completely driven by their minds. He could never make heads or tails of his feelings, even as a child, so he never allowed them to take the reins."

The words clicked in Anna's mind, finishing out the puzzle she had slowly been piecing together since that final night in London. Anna caught Genevieve's eye, and she saw the same understanding settle in her friend and almost-sister's gaze.

Charles likely felt a great deal with regard to Anna, and not necessarily all negative if their conversation and kiss three days ago would indicate. They hadn't had any privacy or opportunity to interact in the days that followed with their family and the final wedding preparations, nor were they likely to until after the ceremony.

She was still rather certain he did not want to marry her, but perhaps his array of emotions, whatever they may be, were too much when he thought of her. And he still struggled, as a grown man, to make heads or tails.

"That is alright," Anna answered warmly. "Charles is free to be who he is, and he is a good, kind, strong man. Those are not small things you are handing me. I am lucky, indeed, and perhaps with time, he and I can grow together. Make each other stronger. I can lead with the heart for both of us, as he can the mind."

The smile melted from Prudence's face, her brow furrowing slightly as she stared at Anna. Then, she took Anna's hands and gave her words back to her. "Of that, I have no doubt."

"Why don't you take the dress off now, dear," Daphne smiled, smoothly shifting them all forward. "I believe it's almost time for luncheon."

"Oh, yes," Prudence dropped her hands and turned to Anna's mother. "Let's give my daughters some time alone to gossip properly before they join us downstairs."

Prudence turned around, winking at Anna before leaving the room. Daphne cupped Anna's cheek with a smile, eyes still soft from seeing her only daughter in her wedding dress, and followed.

Finally, alone for the first time since she arrived, Anna turned to Genevieve. "Well," Anna started.

"It follows his character perfectly," Genevieve said, picking up the exact thread Anna began as she stepped towards her. "Turn around, I'll untie your gown."

Anna had asked her maid, Elsie, to leave after she'd helped her into it since she wanted to see the dress for the first time

with only her family present. It was sentimental, but now she
needed some help, so she did as Genevieve directed.

"It does," Anna agreed. "Truthfully, I began to arrive at a
similar conclusion these past months. Do you recall our last
dinner?"

"How could I forget?"

"When I reflected on it," Anna continued. "That's when it
started to occur to me. Charles is not a cruel or even simply a
rude man. He's the picture of courtesy. And the way he spoke to
me when we were parting…." She paused, not wanting to share
that intimacy. "I think I caught him off guard that night, and
publicly. If he had done that to me, I would have felt all manner
of emotions. I think he did, too. I'm starting to suspect Charles
feels a great deal."

"He was still an ass," Genevieve muttered, finished with
unlacing Anna's dress. Anna went behind the screen to change,
not disagreeing with the truth. "Even so, it does follow. More
than just that dinner, but all of his interactions or lack of interactions with you. He may not be able to quiet his heart when
you're near."

"What a lovely thought," Anna replied, pulling her day dress
back on. "But I would wager it's quite a number of feelings, not
just the pleasant heart-filled kinds, where I am concerned."

There was a pause before Genevieve observed cautiously,
"You are different, Anna."

Picking up her discarded wedding gown, she stepped back
around the curtain to find Genevieve's eyes on her in that too
deep way she had. The kind of scrutiny that rarely missed
anything.

Anna laid the dress out carefully on the bed before turning
around for Genevieve to lace up her dress. She worked quietly,
and Anna knew she waited for a response.

"I want a marriage," Anna finally admitted out loud. "A real
one."

There was a very slight pause in the lacing before Genevieve continued.

"And Charles?"

"It will take time for both of us," Anna offered. "But I have hope we can get there."

Genevieve finished tying her dress, and Anna turned around to find her friend's bow lips pulled up in a grin. "Thank goodness for that."

"I do not want to share this with anyone else, though," Anna informed her. "You and Oliver are our family, but if Charles and I are going to connect, we have to do it our way. Quietly, slowly, privately."

"Of course," Genevieve's gaze turned serious as she looked once more at Anna. "You have my word."

Anna gave her a small smile in answer.

Linking arms, Genevieve started to tow Anna out of the room. "Are you looking forward to the wedding then?"

"I believe so," Anna answered. "But more than the wedding, I am looking forward to our marriage. And our children. I have wanted them for quite some time now. Charles will make a wonderful father."

"And you, a wonderful mother. I hope you both have a child soon." There was a smile in Genevieve's voice as they made their way to the staircase that would lead them to luncheon. "It would be delightful for the cousins to grow up together."

Anna laughed quietly. "I hope we do, too. Your child will have his or her other cousins to grow up with, as well."

"I imagine all the children – Gideon's, yours, mine, Lydia's – will feel like each other's cousins, whether they are by blood or not," Genevieve said sagely. "I am quite grateful we all live so close to one another. None of them will want for company or support as they grow."

The thought warmed Anna. More than just Genevieve and Oliver's children, the Birmingham Estate was within walking distance of Sinclair Manor, and the Coventry Estate not much further. Their children would be surrounded by friends and family from the moment they would be born.

Yes, there was much that Anna looked forward to. And it all began and ended with Charles.

# CHAPTER 16

## CHARLES

"*I*t's finally the day," Oliver broke the silence between them. They sat together at the front of the church, the bright morning light pouring through the stained-glass windows to cast their colors on the dark, holy wood. The soft hum of his friends and family seated around him buzzed like a gnat flying around his head. His palms were sweating but steady, and he resisted the urge to wipe them on the silk clothes of his wedding day.

"It is," Charles replied what felt like stupidly. He didn't really have a reply. All he could think about was the impending hour and the nerves coursing through him.

"You haven't had much time with Anna this past week." Charles could feel Oliver's gaze on him and knew his brother was baiting him into a specific conversation. He didn't have the wits about him to know what, however, nor did he really care when she would soon be here.

"Obviously," the one-word reply hinted more at his irritation rather than a more tactful answer he might have given otherwise.

The past week had gone by faster than any other in his life.

Ever since Charles left Anna in her room after their first kiss, he hadn't had a single moment alone with her, and he was rather grateful for that. Even now, sitting here, waiting to bind their lives together, he still didn't know what to do about her, about them.

Luckily, between the final wedding arrangements, time with their joint families, and the arrival of their wedding guests, they hadn't had a moment's pause long enough to interact.

"Well, we'll all soon be out of your hair," Oliver didn't miss a beat. "Just one more night."

Charles hummed in acknowledgement, but the reality of his brother's words made his mouth dry. Oliver, Genevieve, and his mother were all transitioned to Boncroft Hall as of two nights ago. Anna's parents and the Davenports were the only guests staying at Sinclair Manor, the rest split between Boncroft and the Birmingham Estate, and they would be leaving after breakfast tomorrow.

It had all been carefully orchestrated to give the newlyweds time alone since they did not have a honeymoon planned and soon most everyone would be returning for their Christmas Ball.

Charles heard a commotion at the front of the church, signaling Anna's arrival.

"She's here," Oliver muttered in his ear, standing. Charles watched the priest come forward, signaling for him.

Charles stood and took his position at the altar, his steps unfaltering, hands steady, if a bit moist, as he clasped them before himself. He faced the door at the other end of the aisle and waited.

His heart bounced off the walls of his ribcage, and he took slow breaths of the incense and musk of the church. He could feel the weight of their guests' eyes on him, but it was inconsequential. All he could focus on was the set of large dark wooden doors on the opposite side of the church and the woman standing beyond them.

It felt like both a heartbeat passed and an eternity before the doors finally opened and Anna's best friend, Emily, beamed her way down the aisle. She was a lovely girl, always had been, and clearly a very good friend to his wife. She had often been there in Charles's memories of Anna, her friend so different from his wife in many ways and yet her closest confidant.

Her pink dress added to the young woman's brightness, or perhaps it was the other way around. It was difficult to imagine anything, item of clothing or otherwise, that could dim this woman's vibrancy. Charles found it slightly odd that she had been out for a number of years now and, as far as he knew, had not received any offers.

Not that he would know, if he was being totally honest. It was not as though he talked to his wife enough to hear about the comings and goings of suitors in her friend's life. He didn't even talk to her enough to learn about her own day, let alone someone else's.

Emily reached the altar and took her place.

And then even the air stood still.

Anna stepped into the arched doorway on her father's arm, and Charles stopped breathing. His throat tightened and pressure built behind his eyes as he watched the woman that was the promise of his life step forward. Making her way down the aisle. Making her way to him.

She was the stuff of his dreams. Dreams so grand and great that he had not the luxury to imagine. And yet, she was his. She *was* so similar to him, everyone noticed it, including himself. But more than that, he knew she balanced him. He felt things deeply, far too deeply, and cared, but could never manage to demonstrate it. His warmth a thing hidden within himself while his calm, cool exterior interacted with the world. Anna was warmth. Just as calm, just as composed, and yet she was a soothing balm in a way that he could never be. She made up where he lacked.

That dress was exquisite. White, shining silk, detailed by his mother's hand to her heart's content. He loved Anna for that, he realized, the thought striking him. He loved that she'd let his mother do whatever she wanted to her wedding dress, and she wore it with pride. She honored her. She honored him. And today, on their wedding day, in her wedding dress, carrying herself with such infinite grace as she walked to meet him.... She had never looked more captivating.

Those large crystal eyes held onto him. As if there was no one else in the church. Just him. Just her. And he didn't look away either.

Too soon, not soon enough, Anna reached him. She let go of her father's arm, stopping to accept his kiss on her cheek before taking her place beside Charles. She held a small, simple bouquet of baby's-breath in her hand that balanced the extravagant sophistication of her dress and glittering jewels.

Shit, she was beautiful. Actually, indescribably, painfully, unfathomably beautiful. Had he ever truly noticed before? Truly? She could not possibly be real.

Anna didn't blush, but this close, Charles could see the freckles across her cheeks and nose in detail. He wanted to count them, memorize them, know each and every one of them.

There was something in her eyes today as she looked at him. Something that had not been there the past week in the rare occasions when he met her brilliant gaze. She watched him unflinchingly as though he was all there was in her world, her entire damned universe. As if she actually wanted... no, *needed* him. As if he was her everything, and she was eager, frantic, *desperate* to reach him.

Charles struggled to breathe as he turned from her and faced the priest. Never before had anyone looked at him like that, and it was too much to witness.

The tightness in his throat worsened, and he swallowed past the lump lodged within it.

The priest began speaking, but Charles scarcely heard a word. His body went on autopilot at the strength of the emotions he felt. He actively fought against the overwhelming need to bend over, prop his hands on his knees, and hyperventilate. Instead, he spoke the words required of him when prompted. He heard her answering vows a moment later.

He took his family ring, the one his father had given his mother, and his father's father before him, and so on back into the line of Sinclairs. The ring his son, *their son*, would one day give to his own wife. The son he was required to produce. The son that was the whole purpose of his forced marriage.

Charles placed that reminder on her third finger, her small hand soft and warm in his. Neither one of their hands shook.

And then he was her husband and instructed to complete the first act of his marriage. To kiss his wife.

He finally met her eyes again and once again read the endlessly deep hope there.

Were her eyes smiling? Was she happy? It was hard to tell with those lovely, fantastical lips, which always had that slight upturn to them.

Doing what was required of him, Charles reached a hand up to cup her cheek and noticed the slight hitch of her breath as he bent his head towards hers. He would have missed it completely if he hadn't been so close to her.

His lips met her sweet, full ones. The soft feel of them ignited his blood and pulled at his heart. His fingers twitched against her face reflexively as he fought the desire to grab her with both hands and pull her fully into himself.

Her hand came up and laid over his heart. He knew she could feel its erratic beating just like last time. She surprised him, but of course she did, by letting her tongue out and licking the seam of his lips, wanting entry into his mouth.

Charles pulled back immediately, dropping his hand from her face.

She blinked at him before she collected herself and faced the congregation, taking his arm for him to lead them out. It wasn't fast enough, though. Fast enough for him to miss seeing it again.

*The longing.*

# CHAPTER 17

## ANNA

*A*nna felt like a mess. Since she'd arrived at Sinclair Manor and the progress of that first day, her confidence and positive outlook had only grown. Today, however, her emotions were so intense, she felt incredibly fragile, and she could not understand why. She felt desperate, so desperate for something sweet from her new husband.

*Her husband.* He was her husband now. Yes, he had always been her future husband. But it was no longer 'one day' or 'soon.' It was now. Charles Sinclair was her husband. Now and forever.

And the man could not have pulled away from her fast enough when she tried to kiss him properly.

She smiled at the congregation as she and Charles walked back down the aisle.

She was happy. She knew she was happy. She was *determined* to be happy. But there was an ache within her, too. They respected each other, perhaps even mutually admired each other, and she had always known he didn't want to be shackled to her, but today of all days, she wished for something else. Something more. Something sweet and loving and true.

She didn't notice anyone's face. Not her parents, not her in-laws, not their friends.

Stepping outside, she took a breath of fresh air, the bitter cold jolting her overwrought senses and calming them from the anxious riot of her emotions.

They made their way to the carriage, her arm still linked with his. Her husband's. And then he handed her up into it before following her in.

Anna focused on her breathing, which didn't help as much as it should have since the air was saturated with the scent of pine and forest.

"Anna," Charles's deep voice pulled her attention to where she had it fixed unconsciously to the carriage wall.

"Charles," she replied, meeting his light blue eyes, his expression unreadable. Looking past him out of the carriage window, she saw their guests waving and cheering, and she plastered her faint, polite smile onto her face and waved back as the carriage began moving.

Then, it was just them. For the short carriage ride back to Sinclair Manor, at least. She stared at him as he now kept his gaze averted, watching their progress back to his home. *Their* home.

He had his elbow propped against the door, leaning away from her, as his fingers rubbed somewhat aggressively at his chin. He was brooding. Charles never brooded. He was not a brooding man, and today, he was brooding.

Even still, she had never seen a more handsome sight. She didn't know if it was because it was their wedding day, but seeing him waiting for her at the end of that aisle in his dark, embroidered finery…. His golden blonde hair brushed back, but the errant waves relaxing back into their usual place. His clean-shaven face, his fine aristocratic features, and those sky blue eyes on her. He was the most beautiful thing she'd ever seen, and she wanted to love him. Love him and have him in truth.

"We're married now," she spoke into the silence, her voice quiet and full of the want overtaking her. Want of him, of a proper marriage, of a happy life.

"Yes," he answered in his cool voice, not shifting his position.

"Are you pleased?" She was fishing, blatantly so, trying to pull the answer she was in dire need to hear today. Some sign, even small, that he was glad to have his life bound to hers.

Charles didn't respond, and she took that as his answer. Clearly, it was. She looked down at the small white clusters of her bouquet, clutched limply in her lap.

She focused on the delicate bunches. They were beautiful. Simple and elegant. Her wedding flowers. She traced along one thin branch with her forefinger.

"I think I will keep these," she said softly, really only talking to herself. She didn't have the energy to convince her husband to want to be her husband on the very day he became it. Tomorrow, they'd fall back into place and she'd reestablish her positive conviction, she told herself. But today, she could not bring herself to fight the dejection within herself. "They are not foxgloves, but they are beautiful. I think I will keep them," she repeated, her voice dwindling.

Another few moments passed in silence before the carriage slowed outside Sinclair Manor.

He hadn't said anything. She wished he would. Give her some word of friendship, if not affection, as they embarked on this journey of their life together. Instead, he just opened the carriage door, not waiting for the footman, and exited before holding out his hand for hers. She took it and stepped out.

Charles hooked her hand into the crook of his arm and led her up the stone steps to their lavish home.

Smith opened the door up ahead, his face bright with congratulations as he awaited the new Lady of the Manor. Before they reached within his earshot, however, Charles spoke.

"I am pleased it is finally done with," he said, deflating her chest with his beautiful voice.

She wished he had stayed silent.

THE DAY PASSED IN A BLUR. Their guests joined them for a wedding luncheon at Sinclair Manor before most departed back to their homes. By dinner, they were left with only their close friends, Prudence, and Anna's parents. Anna sat stirring her tea in the drawing room after dinner, still wearing her wedding dress, as she soaked in the heat from the fireplace. The room was lit with the glow of multiple candles that helped her relax after the whirlwind of the day and her own emotional upheaval.

She had calmed as the day progressed, the company of her friends helping remove her from her internal distress. As things felt more normal, she remembered again that Charles was not unkind, nor was he trying to be so this day. It had to have been one of strong emotions for him, too, and more than his words, she let herself accept what he did give her. He had not left her side all day. Truly, all day, until it was time for the ladies to withdraw after dinner. His constant presence; the feel of him beside her; the comforting scent of the woods; the smooth, deep cadence of his voice. It settled her the more the day progressed, and she realized she let herself count on him and his unwavering presence.

Emily, Grace, Genevieve, Amelia, and Lydia all relaxed amongst the couches and armchairs together, relatively quiet under the fatigue of the day. Genevieve yawned, which had Amelia following suit.

"Oh, dear, I apologize," Genevieve said, sitting up.

"Do not apologize," Anna replied, feeling a twinge of guilt at how especially tired the expectant mothers must be feeling. "I'm sure the gentlemen will come through shortly, and we can retire for the evening. It has been quite a long day, but I am so grateful to all of you for being a part of it."

"Of course, darling," Lydia replied. "We hope you both find the happiness you deserve with each other."

"The wedding was absolutely beautiful," Amelia added, smiling softly.

"It was," Emily agreed, reclining into the corner of the sofa, hands lazily clasped in her lap. "You and Prudence did a splendid job with it. And your dress. Anna, I haven't seen anything like it before. It's positively regal."

Anna looked down at the beautiful garment, a smile pulling at her lips.

"Prudence is so talented," Amelia spoke. "I'd love to one day reach her skill."

"I am sure you will, sister," Genevieve said on another yawn.

"You are hardly far behind now," Emily pursed her lips at the duchess.

"How are you feeling?" Grace asked in her quiet way. "Was the wedding to your liking?"

Anna thought back on it. The dress, the church, the man waiting for her. The man whose first words to her after the wedding were not what she had sought, but whose actions were more than what she needed. He may not say the right things, but Charles's actions meant so much more than any said or unsaid words could.

And now he was finally her husband.

"Yes," this time Anna did smile in her usual, composed but happy way. "Yes, I daresay I found it quite perfect."

# CHAPTER 18

## CHARLES

*C*harles was losing his goddamn mind. Which would make sense, of course. The day he finally married; the day he finally lost his mind. He was a complete mix of contradicting feelings and desires. And they were all bloody true.

He made it through the day, however, with perfect composure and decorum. He was certain the tempest within him stayed securely in place, never exposing itself to the outside world. A point proven when after dinner, Oliver, Gideon, Thomas, Alexander, and Jack didn't mention the wedding or Anna. They left him very pointedly alone, purposely discussing politics, Genevieve and Amelia's health and preparations, the upcoming holiday. He'd barely participated, and they did not push him, either sensing he needed peace or that it had been an overwhelming day.

Truly, it had been. After all these years of building up to it, the day itself had been a whirlwind of activity, people, and feelings. The one constant, his one anchor, was Anna. His wife. They stood side by side from the moment she joined him at the altar and weathered the storm of the day together. In fact, the way they felt like a unit today already emphasized his real answer to her question in the carriage. When she'd asked him in a voice filled with the longing he'd seen in the church, his immediate response was he could not have been more pleased. Looking at her lovely, unbelievable face, he felt like the luckiest bastard alive, and that made absolutely no sense.

He had absolutely, unequivocally lost his godforsaken mind.

Now, entering the drawing room, Charles's eyes immediately found his wife seated in the armchair. Even at the lateness of the hour, the persistent length of the day, she still held herself tall and welcoming for their guests. He felt a surge of pride spear through his chest.

Her crystal blue eyes found him, and without thought, his feet began moving in her direction, taking his place beside her. Anna's eyes were unreadable as she watched his approach.

Fuck, he didn't even know what these feelings were that filled his chest to the brim, making it difficult to breathe, but his beautiful wife in her handmade wedding dress sat at the center of all of them.

"Oliver," Genevieve spoke softly, and Charles looked over to find his sister-in-law lifting her head from where she reclined on the sofa to meet Oliver's eyes beside her. His brother understood.

Holding his hand out to her, Oliver said, "Let's go see what raucous Mother is causing in our absence at our new home, shall we, Gen?"

Charles wanted to scoff, and Anna did it for him. Of course, she, too, understood the very obvious truth to Oliver's words. Only a fool would underestimate their mother.

"We shall all accompany you," Gideon announced, which was the cue for the rest of the party. Around the room, the remaining ladies began putting down their cups of tea and getting to their feet.

Charles's heart started pounding.

They'd been together the whole of the day, but as he bid

goodnight to their friends, he was acutely aware that in just a few short minutes, he would be alone with his wife. It would be just them. Just them and just the rest of their lives. The room, which had felt comfortably warm when he first entered, now started to feel borderline stifling. As he escorted the group to the drawing room door, he wished he could follow them outside to breathe in large gulps of the evening air. Instead, he watched as Smith took over escorting them, leaving him alone with his wife.

Charles turned to where Anna now stood next to the chair she'd vacated when thanking and bidding goodnight to their now parted guests. The fire that had him itching to pull at his cravat cast a warm glow over her, glinting off her jewels, and he forgot all the levels of his discomfort as he watched her sparkle before him.

My God, there was no way she was real. That dreamlike beauty lit by the light of the fire in her wedding dress. Her crystal eyes on him, inscrutable and waiting. Her hands clasped before her as they both waited.

Minutes passed.

Finally, Charles spoke, pushing past the dryness he felt in his mouth.

"We should retire, as well," he said, impressed his voice came out even, giving no hint to how his heart raged in his chest. "It's been a long day."

His wife nodded, and Charles held an arm out towards the door, indicating that she should proceed him out of the room.

Anna moved towards him with quiet steps, and he had to swallow at the vision of her walking to him again. She stirred the air with her floral perfume as she led the way into the silent and suspiciously empty hall. It seemed Smith and the rest of their staff intentionally made themselves scarce tonight.

Charles followed Anna to the wide staircase, staying no more or less than a full step behind her. They made their way upstairs and down the hall in silence. When she passed his bedroom door, he stopped, letting her continue to the room next to it. He stood with his hand on the doorknob, the metal cool against his sweaty palm, as he watched her.

She reached her door, extending a hand for her own door-knob, and looked back. She blinked, surprised to find him standing at his door instead of beside her.

Charles moved on instinct – the damnable instinct of self-preservation that reared its ugly head in terrifying, desperate moments and that he had not the slightest chance of subduing or controlling. Once he registered the surprise breakthrough her face, his hand automatically turned the doorknob. A second later, he was safely inside his bedroom, shutting the door, and taking deep breaths to stop his barreling heart rate.

# CHAPTER 19

## ANNA

*H*e was coming.

He was coming, he was coming, he was coming.

Anna repeated it like a mantra as she sat in the center of her bed in a silky, sheer nightgown. The nightgown she had bought especially for tonight, in anticipation of it after their last night in London. She watched the door that separated them, willing Charles to walk through it.

When he had suggested they retire, she assumed he meant together. It was their wedding night after all. Now, they were husband and wife. Of course, they would retire together. But when she reached her door and found him entering his own bedroom, she consoled herself by remembering she had to get ready. He likely did, too.

But as she sat in her expensive, special nightgown, her red hair free and brushed to a gleaming shine down her back, counting the passing minutes with increasing anxiety, she felt a new kind of fear. One she had never once considered or anticipated.

There was no way. There was no way he *wouldn't* come

to her.

Was there?

After what felt like hours but was more likely half of one, she decided she would not torture herself further. Pushing against the soft mattress, Anna shifted to the edge of the bed, tossing her legs over the side. Once standing, she looked down briefly, wondering if she should tie the matching silk robe she wore shut, but decided against it. This was for him. For them. She wanted him to see her. To finally *want* her.

This could be their foundation. If he could want her and be with her this way, coupled with them living together and building a life and family together, one day he would surely, *surely*, want all of her in truth. Would be happy with her. Would be glad to be married to her.

She ignored her pounding heart and strode barefoot to the door connecting her room to her husband's. Lifting her shaking hand, she knocked three times. Steady and firm.

It took a few moments, and yet another new level of terror gripped her that perhaps he would not even answer the door, when it suddenly opened. She exhaled in relief before she could stop herself.

Then, her breath caught.

Her eyes started out on his face. That handsome, elegantly chiseled face she'd loved all her life. His light hair was disheveled, as though he'd been running his hands through it repeatedly, and she found the effect oddly attractive and intimate. The control, the perfect exterior coming undone, and Anna the only one to witness it.

And then her eyes trailed down.

He'd discarded his coat, waistcoat, and cravat, and the top few buttons of his shirt were undone. She followed the column of his strong neck to the golden hint of hair peeking through at the top of his chest. He'd rolled up his sleeves, revealing the muscles of his forearms that she'd always felt beneath his clothing when she held his arm. His shirt was still tucked into his breeches, but without the other layers of clothing, she got a full view of his lean waist and firm thighs, and the growing hardness pushing against the fabric before her eyes.

Anna's mouth watered, and her tongue shot out, licking her lips on instinct before her eyes lifted back up to his face.

But his eyes weren't on hers. They were fixed to the night-gown that hid nothing. Even less so now that her nipples, which had already been visible, had tightened and perked in arousal at the sight of him.

She waited for him to finish admiring her the way she had admired him. Truthfully, it healed something in her that had always questioned if Charles found her physically pleasing. It felt good to see that he was attracted to her and did actually want her in some way. He wasn't as closed off from her as he may seem at first glance. She knew that, but it was still comforting to see.

Anna noticed his hand held onto the door as he looked at her body, throwing the muscles of his forearm in starker relief. She was struck with the most absurd desire to trace them first with her fingers and then her lips.

Finally, Charles met her eyes, his pupils dilated. She fought the urge to pant, her heart was beating so fast at this entire exchange. They hadn't moved or spoken, and she had never felt more aware of her own skin before.

Goodness, he hadn't even *touched* her yet, but her body was preparing for it. Preparing to feel every second of it, becoming oversensitive so as not to miss a single caress.

"Anna," his deep voice was rough, and the sound made a shiver run down her spine.

"Husband," she gave him a nervous smile.

Something flashed in his eyes, but it disappeared before she could identify it.

"What are you doing?" he finally asked.

She blinked. "I...."

For once, she didn't have the right thing to say. What? What did he *think* she was doing? What was *he* doing?

She pulled her shoulders back, lifted her chin, and tried again. "I am seeking out my husband on our wedding night," she replied in an assured voice, completely at odds with the tumultuous nerves skittering within her.

Charles had his reserved, stoic expression back in place, all signs of his earlier shock and arousal erased from his features. She couldn't read what ran through his mind or even try to guess at it. He just stared and stared at her face. But she did not balk. She withstood it, not sure what was going on, but unwilling to back down.

"You're tired," he finally said. "You should rest."

Anna felt her brow furrow as confusion etched onto her face. "I am not tired, Charles. I want to be with you tonight. You are my husband," she said the last as if that was all the explanation she needed to make sense of how nonsensical he was being.

There was another pause.

Then, Charles lifted his gaze over her head before breaking her heart.

"I...," he paused, taking a deep breath. "I can't. Goodnight."

And he shut the door between them.

# CHAPTER 20

## CHARLES

*C*harles reached for his tea, taking a long gulp and wishing it was something stronger. He sat at the breakfast table, the burnt, reddish walls of the room lit by the early morning winter sun shining through the large windows facing the grounds. He forced himself to take a bite of toast that remained dry in his mouth as he chewed.

He had no appetite as he waited for his wife to join him, the memory of last night clinging to him.

Fuck, but she was stunning. That nightgown that was beautiful in its own right and left nothing to the imagination. It fit her perfectly, both in how it draped along her body and the delicate, airy, ethereal quality of it. And the way she wore it confidently as she came to him when he failed to go to her. He had wanted to go to her. He had been pacing his room ever since he entered it, wavering between his desire to go to her and his fear of doing exactly that. She was finally his wife, after all, but he felt the terror clutching him grow the longer he delayed. Terror of what, he could not precisely name, but it was there nonetheless.

Then, his wife had made her move. The image of her

standing proud and elegant and seductive before him, admiring his body openly, getting aroused by the sight of him.... He would never forget that moment as long as he lived.

But even when she pushed for intimacy and connection between them, even with the proof of her arousal and the demanding feel of his own, that terror had him by the throat. He couldn't do it. He couldn't go forward. He wasn't ready. It was as simple and as complicated as that.

And all night, he tossed and turned, a mixture of arousal, guilt, regret, and fear.

Charles heard Anna's telltale soft footfalls a moment before she entered the room.

His wife ignored him so thoroughly, Charles actually thought she hadn't seen him sitting at the table as she walked by it. She went to the side table without breaking her stride, made herself a plate of breakfast, poured a cup of tea, and strode to the table where he sat, taking her seat beside him without a single glance in his direction. He stared at her, shock making him speechless as she pretended he wasn't even there.

She'd never been this cold. His warm, self-assured wife. She was never frigid. In quite literally her entire life, he'd never once witnessed it. Distant, yes. Cold, never.

Anna lifted the cup to her full lips for a sip, and Charles watched her throat swallow, his own body mirroring the action.

"Good morning, wife," he said gently, instinct cautioning him to tread very, very carefully. He'd only ever called her that once before – when she had felt unreachable, some part of him intuitively panicking at the feeling of her being farther than his ability to reach should he want to. Now, her aloofness and his resulting panic were significantly more severe.

"Charles," she replied without looking up, cutting a bite of her food.

Fuck.

"How did you sleep?" He encouraged warmth into his voice, something he found himself only capable of doing with her.

"Well," she lied, taking the bite of her breakfast and not lifting her eyes from her plate. The dark circles under her eyes and the starkness of her many freckles against her skin were answer enough, and guilt seized his chest at the sight.

She didn't offer anything further or ask him the same question.

Charles had known he was making a mistake last night when he shut the door between them, but he had no other choice. He was full of such opposing, overwhelming feelings, and he was terrified. Terrified of her. Of them. Of giving in. Of letting go of the story that was his entire life. Of being with her so completely. Of loving her.

And now he reaped the consequences of his choices.

He fixed a bite his own breakfast on his fork and lifted it to his mouth, not tasting what he knew was a delicious meal. They ate in silence for a few minutes, and the entire time, Charles chewed, drank his tea, felt the warmth of the room, and the panic in his bones.

"What will you do today?" He needed to ask something. He needed to do something. The anxiety coursing through him demanded a remedy.

"I will meet with Mrs. Jaspers after breakfast," she replied succinctly, still not meeting his gaze.

He was struck by a massive sense of loss. His day was about to begin without the light crystal blue of her eyes. They were married now. His everyday should start with the brightness of his wife's eyes.

The guilt eating at Charles multiplied at her response as he chewed and watched her take another delicate drink of tea. When they had still been planning, he had not wanted to take a honeymoon like some happy, in love couple instead of what they were – two people forced together. But now, his wife prepared to set to work the day after their wedding. She was beginning her life as Anna Sinclair not with intimacy and time spent alone with her husband, apart from others and the world, but with his rejection and meeting the housekeeper.

Charles realized just how cruel and selfish his decision not to honeymoon had actually been.

Anna finished the last of her tea, her plate cleaned, and lifted her napkin to wipe her mouth before standing from the table.

Charles said nothing as she left the room without another word.

His wife really hadn't looked at him once. Who knew when she would let him see his favorite color again.

Charles placed his elbow on the table and dropped his head into his hand, rubbing his forehead with his fingers. He lifted his head, propping his mouth against his fist, as he gazed outside the window. The grounds were covered in early morning frost that just started to melt with the aid of the sun, but the coldness in his chest had only grown over the course of the morning.

He'd tried to protect himself last night, to not be crushed by the potent fear that was within him. And in doing so, his first acts as a husband had been to neglect and alienate his wife.

Now, he had to suffer living exactly what he created. All because he had been afraid.

Taking a deep breath, he lifted his head as he refocused his perspective.

This *was* what he wanted for years. To maintain distance between them and avoid the tumult of emotions his wife produced within him. Whether right or wrong; whether he now felt unrelenting panic, regret, guilt lodged in his chest or not – this was the life he had chosen for himself. He only suffered because of whatever these feelings were within him. But he would bury them. He needed to bury them. And eventually, they would disappear.

This was what he had wanted.

# CHAPTER 21

## ANNA

*W*hat an awful start to their married life, Anna thought as she sorted through some of her purchases in her bedroom with Elsie's help. It had been five days since their wedding, and she and Charles had barely spoken. They shared every meal together in relative silence. He didn't come to her at night, and she didn't attempt to reach out to him again.

They had regressed so completely, things feeling even more distant than they had the past years, but Anna could not bring herself to do anything about it. That's what felt so different, she knew. She was so terribly hurt from his rejection that she shut herself off, not even allowing the barest of threads between them. Her ego was still recovering after their wedding night. She had put herself out there, completely and utterly vulnerable, and he had turned her away.

"This looks to be the last of it, Ma'am," Elsie said, holding up a rich burgundy silk dress Anna had purchased for their Christmas Ball.

While she struggled to fall into place as a wife to Charles these past days, she had slipped perfectly into her role as Lady of Sinclair Manor. In fact, she was rather sure her solitude had positively impacted her substantial progress in the running of the house. She had nothing else to do. So, she met with Mrs. Jaspers; met with each of the staff and started to get to know them and their families; planned the menus, the events for the holiday schedule, and where each guest would stay between Sinclair Manor, Boncroft Hall, and the Birmingham Estate. She'd also been able to purchase a few new items for her wardrobe befitting her status as a wife, even if she wasn't really one in truth. No one else knew that outside of Sinclair Manor, though. The decorations were even coming along throughout the house, the feel of the upcoming Christmas holiday adding a kernel of cheer to Anna's heart despite herself.

"I believe there should be matching shoes here somewhere," Anna looked through the mostly empty boxes on her bed before finding the final one. "Here, we are," she pulled her Christmas shoes from their box, and Elsie turned to put the final outfit away in Anna's wardrobe.

"Thank you, Elsie," Anna smiled at the young woman, who was the closest thing to a friend she had in this entire house. Elsie knew that, of course. The whole staff did. Of course, they knew Charles and Anna weren't truly married. That they barely spoke. That they would lead, were already leading, separate lives. Elsie didn't raise the topic, however, allowing Anna to guide what she shared, which was absolutely nothing. She buried the deep shame she felt at her household's knowledge of her failed marriage and ignored it.

Elsie returned her smile and began gathering the discarded boxes on the bed. Once she had hold of them all, she turned back to Anna, "Is there anything else you need, Ma'am?"

"No, thank you, Elsie," Anna went to her bedroom door to open it so Elsie wouldn't have to fight the load she carried. "I will be down shortly."

Anna closed the door gently behind her maid and walked

over to her closed wardrobe. Opening the light wood door, she ran her hand across her new dresses. She'd been careful of how much she'd spent these past few days, both on her wardrobe and for the holidays. Neither Charles, nor the steward she had yet to meet had shared her allowance with her. She'd made sure to make only the necessary purchases for everything in the hopes she did not unknowingly exceed her budget.

She shut the door again and turned around.

She didn't know what to do with herself right now. Everything was fixed, and she didn't want to disturb Mrs. Jaspers just before dinner with yet more holiday planning when they still had three weeks until Christmas. Nor did she want to read or stitch. She loved her new library, but she had already spent an unreasonable amount of time in it over these last five days.

Her eyes snagged on what she really wanted to do.

Biting her lip, Anna stared at the door leading to Charles's room from where she still stood beside her wardrobe.

Charles was likely locked up in his study or meeting with the steward or riding across the grounds. Who knew. He kept himself busy all day, just like she did. It was very easy to see how they would spend the rest of their lives. Separate and quite alone.

Anna hadn't expected the loneliness, not really. Even over the past years when she had stayed on her side of the line between them, she'd never thought far enough ahead to anticipate the deep, aching loneliness that would be the hallmark of the life stretching before her. All the more now that the fear took root within her that Charles may never give her children. But she held on to the hope deep within herself that he was required to. Their whole marriage was predicated on producing a Sinclair son to be the future Earl of Dunhill, so they must.

Damn it, she wanted to see her husband's room.

Lifting her chin, she strode across her own bedroom and opened the adjoining door, stepping through.

The first thing that hit her was the smell. It was him. His scent, only stronger and more concentrated, and Anna felt something tight in her chest ease instantly on the first inhale of the deep, woodsy scent.

She shut the door quietly behind her even though there was no one present to observe her sneaking into her husband's room. She stood still and looked around. The walls were a dark, masculine green, warm and comforting, slightly darker than his study, and the sight of the large, four poster bed made her silly heart pound. The wood of the bed, his wardrobe, and the furniture throughout the room was dark and made with the same fine craftsmanship as hers.

She stepped forward, her footsteps slow as she reached the end of the bed. Wrapping her hand around the carved frame, she continued cataloguing the room. The cold fireplace was set with a pair of dark leather armchairs before it, a small table between them holding a book Charles must be reading. The paintings on the wall were dark, English landscapes that made the room feel warmer and cozier.

The whole space was inviting. Not just for how much it reminded her of her husband, fitting Charles perfectly, but even if she did not know him, this room would feel perfect to her. Perfect to come to at the end of a long day, letting her relax just from entering it, and holding her in its comfort as she fell asleep wrapped in the warmth of the heavy covers.

In another life, Anna would share this room with her husband. Her new dresses would hang beside his clothes in the wardrobe. Her dressing table would be set beside the window. Her book would rest beside his on the small table.

In another life.

In another life, she would not be sneaking in here, days after her wedding, to get a glimpse into her husband's world.

But in this life, she was.

Her chest tightened, and a lump formed in her throat. The

room blurred a bit as she continued to stand in its center, an unwelcome intruder.

She let go of the bed poster and hurried back to their adjoining door, which was dark on his side of it, she registered, matching the style of his room. She shut it quickly behind her and leaned against its cream side. Looking around her beautiful, large, bright bedroom, it felt cold and unwelcoming for the first time. As much as she had been in awe of this space when she first saw it, she now felt loathing fill her at the sight. She hated what this room represented, what it meant. She would be here and never gain entry into the room behind her. The room she loved.

This room shared nothing in common with the one behind her. The room she wanted desperately to be a part of. This was totally separate. Totally other. With a shut door between them.

# CHAPTER 22

## CHARLES

"There's one more matter left to discuss," Geoffrey Perkins, Sinclair Manor's steward said from one of the carved wood and leather seats on the other side of the desk.

Charles had been hiding away in his study more than usual in the ten days since the wedding. He'd shared every meal with his wife, and the panic of her continued silence had yet to diminish. His contribution to the silence, however, was progressing. As the days accumulated, he got stronger at fighting the urge to hear her voice. Rarely did they speak. Even more rarely did she look at him, and he forced himself to live with the profound loss of her. Surely, just a little longer and he would be accustomed to it. He wouldn't wish for her or want her anymore, and these awful feelings within him would finally cease torturing him.

"What is it?" Charles asked, leaning forward and pulling out a clean sheet of paper from the stack on his desk without looking up. He was ready to be done with the man. Perkins was competent in his role of managing the Manor. He'd been raised to it. His father had been the steward to Charles's own father, with Geoffrey taking the reins the last few years of Walter's life.

When Charles took over the household, he thought it a poor reason to rid the man of his livelihood just because he got an odd feeling from him. Charles could never quite pinpoint it, but there was something about Perkins that had always rubbed at him uncomfortably.

"Mrs. Sinclair," Perkins answered, making Charles's hackles rise immediately. His eyes lifted to the thin man before him and narrowed, not liking the way Perkins said his wife's name or the glint in the other man's eyes. He could be objectively decent looking with his dark hair and slim features, but something about his air made him less so. Perhaps it was the arrogance and entitlement. Perhaps it was the ill-intent that always seemed to shine through his beady eyes.

"What about her?"

"She has done quite a bit of spending since she assumed her role."

"And?" Charles did not like Perkins's tone. As if Anna was a willful child or errant worker. *Assumed her role.*

"And she has only been in her position for ten days," Perkins's presumptuous voice made Charles want to punch the man.

Instead, he leaned back in his chair and took a few minutes to simply breathe while his eyes stayed fixed, unblinkingly, on his steward. Once the red had cleared from the edges of his vision, Charles deemed it safe enough to speak.

"*My wife,*" Charles emphasized the words, "is not an employee of this household. She is its mistress. Her *role* is not a position within it, but an owner *of* it. You will adjust your understanding accordingly. Nor does my wife need to limit her spending. If there is anything she wants, she will have it."

The silence following his words was resounding.

Perkins blinked at him with festering eyes. "It seems I have made a misstep. Forgive me."

Charles nodded, his jaw still clenched. He hoped it was not

obvious. Charles was not one to show outward indications of his feelings, but the anger pounded through him at this man's audacity.

He didn't know why the pompous little prick had even brought this up. Charles knew his wife had been shopping. In fact, he was surprised by how modest her spending had been thus far. The accounts reflected the usual holiday spend and an unreasonably small amount to pad her wardrobe. Charles had seen the numbers of what she spent on herself the other day and had to fight the immediate impulse to storm out of his study, find her, and demand she go out and buy whatever the hell she wanted. He got the sense she had only spent the bare minimum needed to present herself as a wife.

And even if she *had* overspent, Charles would not have cared. It would take a good deal for Anna to empty their coffers and send them to the poorhouse, and he knew the type of woman she was, that would never be an issue. And honestly, if she *did* spend enough to bankrupt them, he wouldn't blame her in the slightest after how he'd turned her away on their wedding night. Someone should avenge the pain he'd caused her, especially after she'd taken such care in that nightgown and bravely come to him when he failed to go to her. Hell, she should spend every goddamn cent they had just to make him as outwardly miserable as he was inside.

Regardless, he knew it was Geoffrey Perkins's job to advise him, but his steward should know that Charles kept the Manor in close enough hand to manage his and his wife's spending without input. And where the hell did this man come off looking at his wife's paltry spending and thinking he had any right to speak of it?

Charles thought the matter closed and that the man would take his leave, tail between his legs.

But it seemed Perkins had very little sense as he, too, leaned back in his seat, crossing an ankle over his knee and relaxing as if he sat at a game of cards and not before his employer, and spoke again. "I must have been misinformed. I heard talk within the household that you and Mrs. Sinclair lead rather separate lives for a newlywed couple."

The man had a *death wish*.

This time, the anger spoke before Charles could cool it. "My wife and I are none of your concern, Perkins," his voice came out low and dangerous. "If I hear you speak of her or make any assumptions about her or our marriage, again, I will throw you from this house and ensure no one in this entire country will hire you. Now, *get out*."

Charles had never kicked Perkins out, or really been anything but civil to him, but it satisfied the adrenaline pounding through him to see Perkins snap his mouth shut and hurry to his feet. He nodded his arrogant little head and hurried to the door without another word.

Charles was out of his own chair before the door shut behind him. He prowled over to the side table and poured a drink before tossing it back.

The bastard. Who the hell did he think he was?

Charles poured another glass and took a generous gulp as he paced back to his chair and leaned against it. He stared into the flames of the fire behind his seat, which mirrored the crackling rage within him.

If Geoffrey Perkins didn't have a history with this house, Charles would have fired him on the spot today. He was angry enough at the steward's impertinence, making any comment in regard to his wife's spending, but then the gall of the man to comment on the state of their marriage. *How dare he?*

Never mind that it was true. Never mind that he was also filled with not an insignificant amount of self-loathing that their household already gossiped about his and Anna's marriage. Never mind that it wasn't even really gossip.

He rolled his jaw, grinding his teeth as he willed his heartbeat to relax and his anger to settle. He finished the contents of his glass with the second gulp.

Anna was his wife. She was beautiful, inside and out, and the best woman he had ever known. He would be damned if he let anyone speak, or even think, ill of her.

No one would ever disrespect her, he continued to seethe. *Absolutely no one.*

# CHAPTER 23

## ANNA

"Ah, the elusive Mrs. Sinclair," a deep voice Anna did not recognize spoke from behind her as she reached the staircase in the entry hall. She was on her way to her bedroom to ready for dinner. Glancing behind her, she found a tall, thin man with dark hair and brown eyes. He looked to be in his thirties, maybe very early forties, if she had to guess, and he smiled oddly at her as he came from the direction of Charles's study. She might have even called the look a leer, and it immediately made her uncomfortable.

Turning around fully, she faced the man. "I have not had the pleasure, Sir," she replied. "Who are you?" Her question lacked tact, but something about the way this man looked at her had her guard up.

He crossed the hall and stopped before her, marginally too close. Far enough away not to give anyone pause, but close enough that she felt the hairs on the back of her neck rise. Whoever this man was, she did not like him.

"Geoffrey Perkins, at your service," he gave a little bow, and Anna resisted the curling of her lip as she saw a malicious look spark in his eyes. "Sinclair Manor's steward."

"I am pleased to make your acquaintance," she said in a cool voice. There was something... something that was putting her on edge. The thing behind his smile and his eyes. She knew instinctively that she did not trust this man or want him near her. She took a step back onto the first step of the staircase, angling away from him.

He matched it with his own step forward.

"If you would excuse me, I must ready for dinner."

"I daresay, I had not heard how beautiful you'd be," he ignored her. Anna felt a sudden urge to gag at his words. "I am sorry your husband does not appreciate you."

*What?*

She stopped trying to retreat and faced him fully once more, pulling her shoulders back and looking down her nose at this man that dared speak to her in such a way. Taking a moment to pause, she withheld the words she wanted to say. She did not want to speak so harshly that she caused problems for Charles and the running of the Manor.

"Sir, you are woefully ill-informed," she said in a hard voice. "Nor do I appreciate you speaking to me in such an unsuitable manner. Please leave, and I will not divulge your impertinence to my husband. I trust you can see yourself out."

Without waiting for a reply, she turned on her heel and proceeded to her bedroom. Her hands shook, she realized when she finally shut the door to her room and took a breath, holding them out to be sure before clasping them together to make the tremors stop. She was mostly shaking from anger at the steward's verbal transgression, but also from the residual discomfort at the way he looked at her and the embarrassment she also felt at his words. It was true Charles did not appreciate or want her, and she knew the staff knew, but it was something else entirely to have it said back to her so directly. It was mortifying.

But now was not the time to wallow. There was no time to wallow, she would not allow it. Pushing off the door, she

crossed to the wardrobe to pick out her dress while she waited
for Elsie to come help her prepare for tonight's dinner, which
Prudence, Genevieve, and Oliver would be joining. She wasn't
sure if she was full of relief or dread at the prospect, but she'd
find out soon enough.

ANNA WAITED in the drawing room, seated in the corner of the
sofa closest to the fireplace while she read. She was surprised
from the page, however, when Charles entered. He usually
stayed in his study until dinner was called and then returned to
it immediately upon the end of the meal.

He glanced at her before walking over to the fireplace. She
mentally shook her head as she returned to her book. Of course,
he would join her before dinner tonight, she should have realized. They were expecting guests.

Try as she might, she could not focus on her story anymore.
She read and reread the same paragraph three times before
giving up and placing the book on the table beside her. She
looked up to see Charles already watching her before he quickly
looked away at getting caught.

Anna looked down at her gloved hands in her lap, rubbing
her palms together gently before stilling them. The silence,
which had started to feel normal over the past ten days, felt
especially heavy tonight after meeting the steward for the first
time. She wanted to tell him about it but felt herself hesitating.
It's not like they talked to each other in this marriage.

Before she could overthink it any more than she already had,
heart pounding with nervousness, she spoke, "I met Mr. Perkins
today."

There was a pause and then Charles's deep voice replied,
"Indeed."

She looked up at him. Really looked for the first time since their vows. He was so handsome, it pained something in Anna's chest. The light from the fire and candles made his already romantic, masculine face almost unfathomable to behold. And she saw something soft within his baby blue eyes as he gazed back at her. The part of him she had thought might want her. The part that, even it *did* want her, she now knew would never be powerful enough to outweigh the parts of him that most assuredly did not.

The pressure built behind her eyes, and she lost her composure, having to look away and swallow. She fixed her eyes on the light brown, patterned wallpaper, not really seeing it. It was too much. The hurt from his rejection. The total isolation between them. The desperation for his room, for closeness, for him. The uncomfortable Mr. Perkins. Not being able to tell him properly about the run-in. She missed her home. She missed her parents. She missed Emily. And she was achingly, achingly alone.

Before either of them could say anything else, however, the door opened and Smith showed Prudence, Genevieve, and Oliver into the drawing room.

She stood and greeted her family, glad to feel the relief that filled her at the sight of them. Her eyes began burning again.

What on earth was wrong with her?

She really *was* so lonely, she realized. Of course, she'd known, but she seemed not to have understood how deep that loneliness had already begun to feel.

Prudence took the seat beside Anna, Genevieve on the sofa across from her, while Oliver joined his brother by the fireplace. Their smiles made something in Anna's chest ache further.

"So, my eldest daughter," Prudence reached out and squeezed one of Anna's hands. "How has my son been treating you?"

Awkwardness pulled taut like a string between her and Charles. Unsure if anyone else noticed, Anna replied with her usual small smile regardless, "Very well. How are you enjoying Boncroft Hall, Mother?"

Her mother-in-law's sharp eyes narrowed on her before shifting briefly to Charles. When they returned to her, she asked in her colorful voice, "Is that right?" She posed the question almost like a statement. "Boncroft suits me well," she continued, brushing the question aside quickly with a wave of her hand. "I would like to know, however, has Charles been doting on you as you deserve?"

Those perceptive blue eyes too much like her son's made something want to break in Anna as they assessed her.

"Absolutely," her voice was confident while internally, she felt her already fragile heart starting to fracture. "I have never felt more cherished or loved," she lied smoothly.

Perhaps Anna had felt relief too soon. This was why she had been uncertain if she should dread this evening. Because she didn't want anyone else to know the truth, and she feared she would be unable to adequately hide it.

"Mother," Charles's voice in this moment felt like a dagger to her already bleeding heart. "Leave Anna alone."

Anna glanced to her other side to find the smile had vanished from Genevieve's face. She watched Anna, instead, not with her usual scrutiny but with sadness. As if she didn't need to dig to find the truth. As if she could already see it.

Anna didn't want people's pity. She pulled her lips up further and turned back to Prudence.

"Come now, Mother," she said in what she hoped was an appropriately bright voice. "You must have more to tell us about the new home. You have lived there for a week and a half now, is it to your liking? Have you started preparing the nursery?"

Anna hated to see a look matching Genevieve's flash through her mother-in-law's eyes before she shook her head and covered Anna's clasped hands with one of her own, giving it a squeeze. Then she gave Anna what she asked for – a deflection.

"It's a splendid house," she said. "I find I will be quite comfortable living between there and the Manor until I am ready for my own house and some peace. Until then, I am quite content waiting for my first grandchild at Boncroft, then once you and Charles are expecting, I will make my way back here to help you along, too."

"Mother...." Oliver sighed.

"We all know her plans, Oliver," Genevieve said with a shrug. "She's made very little secret of it from the start."

"Why should I make a secret of it?" Prudence replied. "I intend to be surrounded by my many grandchildren and expect all of you to supply me with them accordingly."

"Heaven forbid we fail to produce," Oliver rolled his eyes.

"Which is why you best start planning for your second now, dear," Prudence advised her younger son. "Once Anna and Charles have their first, I plan to move back to you and Genevieve in time for your second."

Genevieve laughed as Oliver shook his head, lips pursed to hide his amusement.

Anna, however, could not look at Charles or Prudence.

Because with each passing day, it became more and more likely that she would, in fact, 'fail to produce.' Regardless of how much she wanted children, a family, love. Regardless of everyone's expectations around their marriage. She couldn't do it alone. And she was completely and hopelessly alone.

# CHAPTER 24

## CHARLES

*T*his was a ridiculously awful idea.

Charles had been having a difficult day after everything with that bastard Perkins, and then Anna had mentioned she'd spoken to him. Something about the way she brought it up, offering something about an aspect of her day.... He'd been struck by worry and distrust over how Perkins may have spoken to her, and the strongest, most crippling wave of guilt he had felt thus far.

His family had been right all those times they had brought it up before the wedding. His treatment of her, while not ill or aggressive, hurt her. She'd seemed so... wilted. Not just quiet or distant, but like the color was being sucked out of her emotionally.

It had been painful to realize.

Then his mother, Genevieve, and Oliver arrived, and the conversation between her and his mother just made the feeling worse. The performance Anna had been forced to put on that no one bought. The simple questions, the very obvious lies, the smile with which she delivered them.

Charles felt like he couldn't breathe watching it. Like his lungs seized and could no longer expand.

He made it through, conscious of his mother's appraisal, Genevieve's worry over Anna, Oliver's disappointment. They'd trudged through dinner well enough, polite and friendly. Charles was sure his family avoided the topic of their marriage for Anna's benefit more than anything else.

Charles got the sense that Anna was one small step away from breaking.

And he *hated* himself for it.

Anna and Genevieve had just retired to the drawing room, while his mother left for Boncroft Hall, likely to give the sisters time to speak candidly together. Charles was grateful for it. He was now strikingly aware of how alone Anna must be feeling, away from her old home, her family, in a new house, and no one to share anything with, least of all him.

"So," Oliver broke into the heavy silence, their brandy before them, cigars in hand. The warmth of the candlelight and red walls felt like a blanket around them. Charles lifted his gaze from where he'd been staring unseeingly at the white tablecloth while he'd been drowning in his guilt. His brother leaned back in his chair and raised his cigar as he sized Charles up. He took a puff before continuing, "What's been going on, Charles?"

Charles dropped his eyes to his brandy, reaching his free-hand forward to spin the crystal tumbler in circles on the table-cloth as he answered, "What do you mean?"

"How is married life so far?" Oliver made no assumptions, nor did he let his frustration show when he obviously knew things were still not well between Charles and Anna. It was the first time Charles could recall him simply asking rather than pushing Charles to be better.

It made him feel worse. Like Oliver had finally accepted that Charles was a hopeless case.

"As expected," Charles lifted his glass and took a swig,

wishing the brandy burned more. Wishing it hurt the way his heart had been hurting all evening. Wishing it would distract him from the pain of it.

"Is Anna settling in?" Oliver's eyes were a solid weight upon Charles.

"It would seem so," Charles matched his brother's posture. "In ten short days, she's managed to get the running of the Manor in hand, met and talked to each of the staff, and planned much of the Christmas celebrations. The decorations are even beyond what Mother used to do, as you saw. There's a garland or wreath on every surface, and you see the trees. She has one in every room." He lifted the cigar to his mouth, an ember of pride momentarily taking dominance within him over his tumultuous emotions from the evening. His wife had done well. So splendidly well, and he *was* proud of her. She'd assumed her new responsibilities and their household with grace, confidence, without complaint – not that he gave her the opportunity or welcome to share anything, complaint or otherwise, with him.

"I did," Oliver nodded, looking away from his brother. He glanced at Charles before reaching for his brandy. "The house has never looked more beautiful, even Mother said so when we arrived." Oliver paused the glass he held halfway to his mouth. He seemed to weigh his next words as he still kept his gaze averted. "It's quite a lot to accomplish in a week and a half, especially as a fresh newlywed."

The implied question fell between them, a heavy thing resting beside the holly floral arrangement in its lavish gold vase between the large, matching candelabras on the table.

"She is quite exceptional," Charles evaded the question with honesty, unable to express the turmoil rampaging through him.

"I have not the slightest doubt," Oliver said before finally asking directly, "And has she spent much time with you these ten days?"

"Every day," he answered, puffing his cigar without hesitation or any indication of how his throat felt like it had fallen into his chest. It was a childish version of the truth. He knew what Oliver asked, and his brother did not mean the silent daily meals Charles and Anna shared together.

Oliver and Charles stared at each other from across the table, and then it seemed the regular frustration Oliver held at bay tonight finally won out. He leaned forward and stubbed out his cigar, shaking his head. Charles did the same, cautiously watching his younger brother as he reached for his tumbler and tossed the remainder of its contents back.

"You're a goddamn liar," Oliver ground out. "And Anna is unworthy of your disregard. You should have called off the wedding if you were going to toss her aside as carelessly as you are."

"I couldn't call off the wedding," Charles replied, trying to slip into his cool, matter-of-fact demeanor, but he worried it fell rather flat. "Nor have I tossed her aside. I am here, she is here. We have been and will continue to live together."

"If you had told her father how you intended to treat her, I am sure he would have let you out of Father's promise." Oliver glared at him as he stood up and continued, "He, unlike you, loves that woman and understands what she deserves in life. That was *why* he gave her to you. And you have absolutely cast her off. A shared roof does not alter that."

Oliver strode from the room, leaving Charles seated at the table. All of what Oliver said was likely true, Charles thought as he, too, gulped down the last of his brandy and stood from the table to follow his irate brother towards the drawing room.

But it was more than just the bargain between their parents that prevented Charles from calling off their wedding. The truth of it was, either as a direct result of that arrangement or otherwise, Anna had always been his, and he had always been hers. Forced or not. Bitter or not. That was the truth. *That* was the reality. Anna had always been his wife. There was no one else.

He couldn't have called it off.

There had never been anything to call off.

# CHAPTER 25

## ANNA

"*How* is everything?" Genevieve asked gently, taking the cup of tea Anna handed to her, the light from the fireplace beside them reflecting off the gold detailing on the cup.

This night had been exhausting, and Anna felt the lie too much effort to speak as she returned her focus to the tea tray to pour her own cup.

"Likely exactly how you expected," she replied.

"He still hasn't warmed to the marriage?" Genevieve asked, stirring her tea as Anna leaned back on the sofa beside her and did the same in an attempt to cool the beverage.

"I am beginning to doubt he ever will," she softened the truth. She knew most assuredly now that Charles would never warm to their life together. Not that they really had one, but any delusions she'd previously held that they might were fast disappearing.

"What happened to your desire for a real marriage?" Genevieve's brow furrowed. She seemed to have forgotten her tea, but Anna took a sip of her own as Genevieve pushed. "Has something happened, Anna?"

"Nothing has happened," Anna replied, not bothering to fully explain that when she said nothing, she meant *nothing*. Not a single thing had happened between them. Intimate or otherwise. And the reality of that had completely disillusioned her.

The insidious thought that had been gathering power in Anna's mind the past week and a half, even as she tried to ignore it, almost made its way out. She had begun to wonder if their problems went beyond Charles not wanting her. Maybe... maybe he wanted *someone else*. He had spent so much time in London before the wedding. Perhaps it had been because someone still pined for him there and he for her.

Genevieve would know. If Charles had left to meet with another woman while she and Oliver lived with him before the wedding or if he maintained correspondence with someone.

The question made its way to the tip of her tongue, but she took another sip of tea to thwart it. She would not embarrass herself with such a question. Or its possible answer.

"Anna...," Genevieve started, her voice trailing off. Anna kept her eyes on her sister-in-law, unwilling to show things were amiss more than was already apparent. Before she could continue, however, Oliver tore open the drawing room door, pulling both of their gazes to him as he strode angrily into the room and directly to Anna, taking the seat on her other side.

"I am sorry, sister," he looked at Anna's shocked face, his dark blue eyes, so different from his brother's, blazing with poorly suppressed fury. "Please, accept my sincerest apologies on behalf of my brother and my family. You are an exceptional woman and deserve much better than my foolish brother's treatment of you. While he may not appreciate your worth, *we* do. And if you ever find yourself in need of space, Boncroft Hall is another one of your homes. You need not send word ahead or provide any explanation, and you have every right to live with us for as long or as short a time as you wish. You need no one's permission to do so."

Anna stopped breathing. Her throat felt thick, and pressure built behind her eyes at the abrupt and heartfelt words. Genevieve must have noticed because her hand grasped Anna's where she still held her cup in her lap.

Charles walked in, his expression closed, and Oliver ignored him completely. Anna got the sense Oliver wanted to strike his own brother.

"It's true," Genevieve whispered.

Oliver remained focused on her, and Anna realized he waited for her to reply. She still couldn't speak past the lump in her throat, but she managed a nod, and the sadness she read on Oliver's face did not feel like pity. It felt like an apology. One she felt he did not owe her, but she appreciated nonetheless. More than that, she believed him. They were Charles's family, but they were hers, too, and Oliver and Genevieve were telling her she had their support. Knowing that and that she had somewhere she could go, even if she likely never would.... Well, it made her feel just a little less alone.

He returned her nod, satisfied that she understood the import of his words and turned to his wife. "Gen, we should likely return home."

Genevieve nodded, placing her cup back on the tray atop the small table. She leaned over and kissed Anna's cheek before she and Oliver made their exit.

Once they were alone, Anna finally looked at her husband where he stood behind the armchair closest to the drawing room door. She expected him to make his retreat now that the night was over, but when she met his eyes, she saw surprise flit across his fine features before he moved.

He took Genevieve's vacated seat, but he sat much closer to her. The proximity, the way he faced her, the quickness with which he'd come to her echoed of a familiarity they did not possess with one another, and that just saddened her further. She struggled to breathe without giving into the sobs that demanded escape from within her. She hadn't cried. In all the days since the wedding, through all the heartache and loneliness, she had not shed a single tear, and now, she was breaking from the pressure of continuing to hold everything in.

Charles reached one of his beautiful hands out to hold her gloved one, now empty since she discarded her cold tea with Oliver and Genevieve's exit. Anna looked down to see the long, elegant fingers clasping her gently, and her breathing hitched on a silent sob.

"Anna," he whispered in that low, warm voice he only ever used with her the very few times she'd heard it. "Are you alright?"

She couldn't suppress the mirthless chuckle that his question pulled from her, one of the sobs threatening to overtake her releasing with it. "Am I alright," she repeated in a whisper to herself, still looking down at their joined hands in her lap, shaking her head. This was the first time he'd ever held her hand. Eighteen years of an engagement, ten days of a marriage, and this was the first time her husband had ever held her hand.

"Are you in love with someone else?" The question left Anna of its own accord, as if her mind and body could no longer contain it, regardless of her wishes, with all the emotions tearing her apart.

"What?" The shock of his voice had her looking up. He was so beautiful. The firelight glowing off his light-yellow gold hair and pale blue eyes, casting shadows on those delicate, sharp angles. He could have been an angel. And she was so exhausted, so distraught as she observed him, the worry on his handsome face, she couldn't even feel the shame when the tears built up over days, over a lifetime, began to overflow slowly from her eyes. Charles's face contorted with what looked like pain at the sight. "Anna, there's only ever been you."

Her hands shook, but she couldn't think of something to

reply. She didn't believe him, she realized. How could there only be her when he did not want her?

He seemed to hear her disbelief in the silence because the hand that held hers tightened its hold while his other hand reached up and cupped her cheek, wiping away her tears. "I've been promised to you since I was ten, Anna. I've never loved or been with anyone else. I have only ever been yours."

Anna lost what little hold she had on herself and dropped her head, her eyes shutting as a proper sob left her. Her chest and shoulders shook as his words caused her heart to seize, wishing it was the truth.

Charles's fingers curled under her chin and lifted her head back up, prompting her to meet his eyes again. His eyes were agonized, his brow pulled down in dismay, as his thumb stroked her face.

He seemed to see her continued doubt without her having to say it, so he repeated in that deep, intimate, infinitely warm voice that belonged only to her, "Only yours, Anna. There has never been, nor will there ever be, anyone but you for me."

And then her husband leaned forward and sealed his lips to hers.

# CHAPTER 26

## CHARLES

*C*harles kissed her, his desire, guilt, pain, shock channeling through and making the kiss all the more tender. He could not believe he had created such a situation that she would *doubt* what he was to her. He might not have chosen it, he might have been stubborn about it, but how could she for one iota of a second think that there could ever be someone else? She was his whole life, and he was hers. She likely couldn't remember a time not being betrothed to him, nor could he scarcely do so, and yet she thought he was not hers? That he might be another's? He had not anticipated that reaction, and the shock of it, as well as watching her all night trying not to break only to fall apart now, rocked him.

He angled his head and licked along her lips like she had on their wedding day, and unlike him, she opened for him. His tongue connected with hers in a gentle, quiet dance that made heat scorch through his veins. Steady and overpowering. He could taste the salt of her tears, and it broke him.

He could not bear to see her cry. In eighteen years, he'd never once witnessed it. She'd always been so together, so poised. To see the turmoil of the past week and a half, topped with today, defeating her.... They were all right, his friends, his family. Anna was sweet and kind and wonderful, and he was hurting her. She deserved better from her husband. Watching her lose the hold on her composure, watching the tears spill down her face.... It destroyed him utterly.

And then there was that question. She didn't believe him when he told her he was hers, and truthfully, why should she, when all he had done was show her the opposite?

He couldn't let himself do this to her anymore. He *would* not. He had caused this. He made her doubt him. He had brought her to her breaking point – strong, assured, brave, beautiful Anna. To hell with what he thought he wanted – distance and an end to the storm of his feelings. Damn his feelings. He would never make his wife cry like this again. Absolutely never.

Anna reached the hand not gripped in his up and wrapped it around his wrist. He deepened the kiss, and his cock, which had already been hardening, turned to granite as he heard and felt her quiet, delicate moan.

God, he still wanted her. She was so exquisite. Not just her beauty, the soft skin beneath his fingertips, the body he'd glimpsed but not enough. She was strong, intelligent, and graceful. She took his own inner turmoil and neglect in stride and had still been a perfect wife in spite of it. She was brilliant. And he was an undeserving bastard.

His blood roared within him, his heart pounding as the desire began to outweigh everything else between them. He needed her closer. Moving both hands down, he used one to grab her waist and brace her back, while the other went to her thigh, and he pulled her up into his lap without breaking their perfectly balanced, sweetly passionate kiss. His heart glowed, the feeling both painful and wonderful, at the tenderness of their passion. He could feel how it would be between them, and it was everything he wanted and did not deserve.

She wrapped her arms around his shoulders, her body trembling slightly in his arms, as if she felt exactly what he did. It was powerful, the thing between them, emotionally and physically.

He lifted the hand from her thigh back to her face and stroked her cheek before he cupped the back of her head gently, lacing his fingers in the strands of her soft copper hair. The fire continued to build from their unending kiss. He wanted to touch her, fill his hands with the shape of her, memorize every dip and curve. He wanted to feel her skin against his, to see her, fill his eyes with each naked inch of the body that had teased him in that beautiful silk nightgown.

But he couldn't tonight. He had done too much damage to do anything more than kiss her, hold her, show her who he belonged to.

Her floral scent was a drug, and combined with the feel of her full lips, sweet taste, and tender movements, he lost himself completely to her and wished never to be found again.

It was Anna who, moments, maybe seconds, maybe days, later pulled her mouth away from his, panting softly, and rested her forehead against his shoulder. Charles kept his hand on the back of her head and used the other to trace her spine in soothing strokes.

Her hands had lowered to his chest and one of them clutched the expensive fabric of his coat as they sat there, absorbing each other. He was still hard against her leg and would certainly remain so for some time yet, but tonight was most definitely not the night to progress things physically. Not with all the damage coming to the surface between them and everything yet unresolved.

Charles kissed the top of her head as their breathing slowed. He kept his lips against her as he whispered in a voice roughened by his arousal and guilt, "I am only yours, wife. Since I was ten years old, I have only been yours."

"I don't understand," her quiet words broke, and Charles's chest seized at the sound.

He rested his cheek atop her head and wrapped both arms around her, holding her as the regret crippled him.

"I know," he told her. "But it is still the truth. And it's my fault you cannot see it."

He heard the quiet sniffle that she tried to hide, and he tightened his hold on her. He breathed in her flowery scent, letting it fill his lungs and saturate his blood. At one point, she turned her face towards his neck and laid her cheek against his shoulder, and he kept his head resting atop hers. He stared into the fire, watching the logs burn and fire crackle under the garlanded mantlepiece. They sat that way for long minutes. And even with all the issues he had yet to face and expunge, even with the damage and questions sitting heavily between them, even with the pain and hurt they still had to heal, he was overwhelmed by a deep sense of contentment as he quietly held his wife.

Eventually, Anna lifted her head, and he unwillingly released her. She looked at him, her tears dry, but the redness of her eyes a knife to his chest. She watched him for a moment before speaking.

"I don't know what this is tonight," her voice was once again the solid, sure thing he was used to. "I don't know how you will be tomorrow."

Charles swallowed and nodded because he understood. She didn't trust him to care for her because he hadn't been. Or rather, he had been, because he always cared about her, more than anyone else in his life he cared about her, but he had refused to show it.

"I should retire," she said, gathering her skirts and standing up.

He felt the loss of her touch acutely.

"I will walk you to your room," Charles responded quickly, standing up.

She looked up at him, and the thought was clear – he hadn't

walked her to her room since their wedding night, when he'd rejected her and left her to sleep alone.

Taking her hand, he pulled her out of the drawing room, across the silent entryway, and up the staircase. They reached the upstairs landing when Anna spoke.

"You've never held my hand before tonight," she whispered.

He turned his head and looked down at her. She faced straight ahead as they proceeded down the hall in the direction of their bedrooms. She hid it in her voice and expression, but Charles sensed the hurt behind her observation.

There was nothing he could say. So, he lifted her hand to his lips and kissed her knuckles.

She glanced up at him, and he noticed the slight twitch at the edge of her gorgeous lips. He hoped that meant she understood his apology and promise.

This time, Charles walked her all the way to her door, passing his own. He paused outside it, and she turned to him, her crystal blue eyes wary as they met his. Was she nervous he'd try to spend the night with her? She needn't be. When they finally made love, he would do so as the man and husband she deserved and without anything but joy and love between them. Not pain. Not neglect. Not even the damned expectations from their families. It would be them, and them alone. And right now, they had some work to do before reaching that point.

Still holding her hand, he lifted the other to cup her jaw as he bent down and kissed her lips. Ten days married, and this was the first time he kissed his wife goodnight.

"Sleep well, wife," he murmured against her lips.

She met his eyes, her gaze more assessing now, before she filled his heart to bursting with her reply.

"Goodnight, husband."

# CHAPTER 27

## ANNA

*A* good night's sleep did wonders for Anna, as did letting her tears out. She woke the day after the family dinner still weighed down by her emotions, but they did feel somewhat lighter. And then there was Charles's behavior from the previous evening. The way he had cared for her, held her, kissed her. The things he had said. It seemed unbelievable that he had considered himself hers for the past eighteen years, even now, but in the bright light of day, fully rested, she wondered if it might be true.

Anna made her way down the stairs, her hand light on the intricately carved banister and careful not to disturb the garland wrapped around it, and wondered what she should expect from her husband today. If he would continue to be closed off or if last night really was the breakthrough for them that it felt like.

Feeling oddly nervous, she reached the main floor and stepped towards the dining room for breakfast. She made sure to keep her face neutral and not get her hopes up since there was a very real likelihood that the walls between them would be thicker than ever this morning.

"Good morning, wife," Charles smiled, *actually smiled*, at her as she stepped into the bright dining room, whose red walls looked almost ablaze in the bright winter sunlight pouring in through the windows.

Anna was so surprised by the greeting that her steps faltered just inside the door.

Her mind quickly shot through her options as his blue eyes watched her warmly. She could protect herself from the risk of getting burned by his disregard once again. Or....

"Good morning, husband," she replied, trying to be receptive but unable to smile or fully subdue the wariness in her tone.

His gaze softened as if he heard it and understood.

What in the world?

She felt her brow pinch slightly as she stepped into the room properly, heading to the side table to fill a plate with breakfast. Anna focused on her routine, but she could not fully ignore the heat of his gaze on her as she took her seat beside him, the very different atmosphere in the room. It felt... open. And it made her heart flutter.

"How are you this morning?" he asked, the concern evident in his voice.

Anna didn't pause as she picked up her fork and began putting together her first bite, glancing up at him and answering honestly, "Much better."

"I am relieved to hear it."

They ate in silence. Anna considered asking him how he was as she chewed her eggs, but she couldn't do it. She was able to acknowledge and accept his attempts at reaching out, but when she thought of putting herself out there again.... She just couldn't do it, yet. Even if she wanted to.

"How did you sleep?" Charles's voice broke through her internal debate.

Lifting her head, she observed his eyes on her again. She realized what felt so different in his gaze today. It was the same as last night. The soft, sweet part of him that she sometimes thought may want her. It shined through, confident, transparent, and unhesitating.

"I had some trouble falling asleep," she replied, her eyes riveted to the expression in his gaze. Unmoored by it. "But once I did, it was quite restful."

He nodded, and the remainder of their breakfast continued similarly. Charles asking questions, Anna's responses forthcoming. It was awkward and stilted, but also the most they had conversed since their wedding day. It was as if a thread extended between them now. Fragile and tenuous. Easily broken.

But it was there. Stretching from her to him, and they each held on to their end.

Anna didn't know how to strengthen it or how to keep it from breaking. But she held on tight to her side and started to feel the flickerings hope bloom within her once again over their meal.

For two more days, Charles and Anna continued to attempt conversing with each other as they ate. Charles had even insisted for the first time that Anna no longer sit at the opposite side of the table like she usually did during their evening meals. He wanted her in the seat next to him, which she occupied during their breakfasts and luncheons.

The hope in Anna strengthened with each interaction. She kept waiting for the walls to erect themselves within his eyes, to feel the coldness of the distance between them, but it never appeared. And with each passing exchange where Charles looked at her with something like affection and warmth, and spoke in that low tender voice, she started to trust it just a tiny bit more. He had even told her today as he left to go to Boncroft

Hall to see his brother. He'd never told her when he left home for anything before.

Anna was still cautious, of course. Not putting herself out there too much yet, afraid to say too much and tear that thin thread between them as it slowly thickened. But there was hope there, too.

She smiled as she adjusted the holly arrangement on the center table of the entry hall. The holiday decorations had come along splendidly. Wreaths on every door. Holly and greenery artfully arranged on every table in detailed gold vases and matching candelabras. Garlands wrapped around every banister and mantlepiece. Now, she awaited the large tree the staff would bring in shortly for pride of place in the entry hall, which they would then decorate to finish out the holiday décor. She had a few smaller trees in each of the rooms within the Manor, but this would be *the* tree. The Sinclair Manor Christmas tree.

As she waited, Anna critically assessed the arrangement on the table before her and decided to make a few changes to get it absolutely perfect. She pulled out a sprig of holly and started to shove it back into the vase a little lower. Pulling her head back slightly and squinting, she noted it was too close to another piece and pulled it back out again, moving it just slightly farther up.

"My dear, Mrs. Sinclair," an unwelcome voice interrupted her concentration, making her hackles rise. "How lovely you look today."

With everything going on between her and Charles, she'd forgotten about Geoffrey Perkins. She turned towards the front door to see the evil looking steward walking towards her. She didn't know if he actually looked evil or if her previous interaction with him colored her judgement, but she stood by it, regardless.

Her eyes glanced around the empty hall. Apart from propriety's sake, something about this man made her not want to be alone with him. She hoped Mrs. Jaspers and Elsie would return quickly with the ornaments they'd gone to gather.

"Mr. Perkins," she said in an aloof voice. "Good afternoon. My husband is not presently at home. I will let him know you stopped by."

"So quick to run me out the door, my dear?" If he was trying to sound teasing, he failed miserably as his words came out slimier than anything else.

He had come to a stop in that same just far enough, yet still too close way as last time, and Anna adjusted her angle slightly to give herself more room. She recalled from their previous interaction how an obvious step back had prompted him to close the distance.

"I would remind you, Sir, that I am the Lady of this house," Anna spoke firmly, her eyes cold on the man's face. She gave no outward indication of how nervous she felt and how uncomfortably her heart raced. She was glad her practiced composure kept the sprig of holly steady in her grasp. "And a married woman. Your words and attentions are wholly unwelcome and inappropriate, and I must ask you to cease them at once."

"What a tease you are," he snickered, and Anna's lip curled in disgust as she looked at him. "As if your marriage was anything to safeguard –."

"You will leave now, Mr. Perkins," Anna interrupted in a hard voice. "And you will only return when my husband is present so that you may conduct your business with him directly. Good day."

He barked a laugh, and Anna's terror grew the longer they were alone. What if he did not leave?

"Are you sure –," he began, but thankfully, the door opened on the far side of the hall. She saw Smith appear, helping Mrs. Jaspers and Elsie carry in boxes of ornaments for the tree.

"Smith," she sighed. Anna's relief was potent as she stepped towards the approaching trio. Her hands finally started to shake, but she masked it with her confident stride across the hall towards them. Taking the box out of Smith's arms, she continued, "Mr. Perkins requires some assistance finding his way out. Could you please help him?"

Smith's eyes narrowed on the steward, his distrust and dislike evident. It was furthered by the low tone he used when he replied, "Of course, Ma'am." He stepped towards the younger man and escorted him out, but not before the steward threw a nefarious smile in Anna's direction where she still stood next to the other women.

"What a horrible man," Anna heard Mrs. Jaspers spit. "He makes many of the young ladies of the house uncomfortable with his leers and overfamiliarity."

"I do not doubt it," Anna commented, watching his exit and trying not to let the depth of her unease show.

"Are you alright, Ma'am?" Elsie asked softly.

"I'm fine," Anna turned and gave her a small smile, happy Geoffrey Perkins was no longer in her home. "Come, let's get these sorted before the tree gets here," she said and led the way back to the center table to finish up her Christmas entry arrangement and prepare for her first official Christmas tree in Sinclair Manor.

# CHAPTER 28

## CHARLES

*C*harles finally swallowed his pride and rode his horse the short, cold ride to Boncroft Hall. It had been three days since his family joined them for dinner at Sinclair Manor, and since then, he reached out to Anna during their shared meals, sat with her before and after, made stilted attempts at conversation, but it still was not easy.

The brisk wind tore at his face until he finally came to a stop before his brother and sister-in-law's new home. It was smaller than Sinclair Manor, but the architecture was more extravagant with its stone pillars and intricate detailing. As he made his way up the steps and inside, a footman opened the door and Davies stood just inside to greet him. Since Charles no longer stayed at Sinclair House in London year-round, Davies had abandoned his post there to support the younger Sinclair couple at their new home.

"Is my brother at home?" Charles asked after returning the greeting and removing his winter cloak and passing it to the footman.

"Yes, Sir. He is in the study with His Grace, the Duke of

Birmingham," Davies replied, turning and already leading the way in that direction.

The entryway was white with detailed trim and pillars mirroring the outside architecture of the home. Oliver and Genevieve had decorated with dark wood furniture that perfectly balanced the place and matched the bannisters of the wide staircase that led upstairs.

"Are you enjoying country life, Davies? It's rather different from our time in London," Charles commented, falling into step beside him.

"Indeed, Sir," Davies smiled at him. "But it suits me well, and we are all very pleased to see you finally settled home."

"You never shared your concerns otherwise before," Charles challenged.

"It was not my place," Davies all but shrugged.

"Somehow I doubt that would have stopped you," he replied honestly.

Davies didn't bother hiding his chuckle. "That is likely true, Sir," he said. "Perhaps it is more apt to say it was not the time to voice my concerns previously. You seemed to need the separation of Sinclair House for the time we were there. It would not have helped to tell you otherwise."

That was precisely why Charles had stayed in London for the better part of the past few years, only visiting Sinclair Manor when duty called. He needed the separation. To hideaway until he was forced to return. Return and run the Manor with his wife.

But he wasn't here to dwell on the past or what he had been forced into. He was here to focus on the future and no longer fight what he wanted, regardless of how it came to be.

A moment later, Davies led Charles through a door and announced him before exiting again. Oliver, Gideon, and his son, George, sat at a table by the large window across the room, engaged in a game of cards. The room was paneled with light wood, and a fire crackled under the pale mantlepiece on the wall perpendicular to that of the large windows. Charles crossed the space, passing the desk closer to the door, and the light blue and brown seating arranged in the center of the room.

"Charles," Oliver glanced at him before reviewing his hand again. "I did not expect you. Pour yourself a drink," he said while also reaching a hand forward to hold up his own empty tumbler. Gideon, too, lifted his empty glass for a refill with a muttered greeting.

Charles pursed his lips but took the crystals from their hands to the side table, refilling their glasses and pouring one of his own. He held theirs in one hand as he returned to the table, taking a sip of his as he walked.

All three occupants of the table had cards in their hand, including the almost two-year-old George, who was the spitting image of his mother.

"Apologies for not sending word ahead," Charles replied, placing their tumblers between them and taking a seat opposite Gideon at the round table, Oliver and George on either side of him.

"You didn't need to send word," Oliver spoke absentmindedly. "It's probably good you didn't since Mother would likely have prepared herself to tear you to shreds if she'd known you were coming. She's quite cross with you, also, after dinner the other night. Regardless, I am inquiring after what has brought you here. I thought you and Anna couldn't make it."

"Anna?" Charles asked, distracted from his purpose, his brow pulling down.

At this, both men looked at him. "Yes," Oliver replied, watching his brother carefully. "Her Grace –."

"Amelia," Gideon interrupted.

Oliver corrected himself as if this was a normal occurrence between them, which it was, and continued, "Amelia is with Genevieve and Mother. They were having tea and then putting the final touches on the nursery. Mother and Amelia finished the blanket they stitched for the baby, too, which they wanted to add to the room."

"Not that the child will get much use out of it," Gideon added. "They've put so many stitches upon stitches onto that blanket, it will likely irritate the child more than anything. Be sure to get a proper blanket for the baby to actually use, Oliver."

"I am sure we have no shortage of things for the baby," Oliver answered as they returned to their cards.

"What about *Anna*?" Charles tried to refocus them.

"She was invited," Oliver glanced at him again before quickly looking away. "She said she did not feel well."

But she hadn't been ill. She seemed fine at breakfast and had even smiled at him, not mentioning anything, when he'd told her he was coming here. He didn't blame her, of course. It was his own doing, and while she'd been receptive of his solicitations, she was still wary. Only responding, not risking anything or reaching out to him again. That was why he was here now.

"I imagine it would have been quite difficult for her," Oliver continued in that same careful voice.

"What would?"

"Joining two happily married, expectant mothers for tea to discuss a nursery." As soon as Oliver said it, Charles recognized the obvious truth.

He'd created such an unhappy marriage for her that it would upset Anna to spend time with her own friends and see how happy they were in their marriages.

*Shit.*

"I need your help," Charles cut to the chase, heart pounding slightly.

"Oh?" The two men continued to play together as George played happily beside them with his own cards.

"I want to fix things with Anna," he forced out.

"Fucking finally," Gideon muttered, not looking up.

"But I don't know how."

"What do you mean, you don't know how?" Oliver asked.

"Exactly what I said," Charles gritted out, the irritation building up within him. "I've tried talking to her more the past few days, asking her about her day, the house, her planning, and she's been receptive, but... it's still difficult between us. And she isn't offering anything. She answers me, but she doesn't reach out herself anymore."

Gideon gave an unamused chuckle. "How ironic," he supplied, causing Charles to glare at the duke.

"Have you tried doing things with her?" Oliver asked.

"Like what?"

"Like go for walks, ride around the grounds, go for a picnic," Oliver said as if it were obvious and Charles was an idiot.

"It's the middle of winter."

"And you have cloaks," Oliver countered. "And have a picnic inside."

"That's ridiculous." Charles wanted to roll his eyes.

"Be ridiculous," Gideon returned. "You can't deny you've neglected her for months now. If you need to be ridiculous to fix it, *be ridiculous*, damn it."

"Damn it," George cried amidst his toddler babbling.

"George," Gideon's tone was hard as he scolded his son. It would have made any grown man's back straighten, but the little boy just giggled in his father's face. "Amelia's going to love that," Gideon groaned.

"You never courted her, Charles," Oliver explained to Charles. "You have to court her, even if you are married. Get to know her. Spend time with her for no other reason than to spend time with her. You didn't even have a honeymoon. But you can still give yourselves one together at the Manor. That's why we all left."

Could it truly be so simple?

"Talk to her after you've been intimate together, too,"

Gideon suggested. "Hold her and talk to her. That's when you two are closest physically, and it's the perfect opportunity to grow closer in other ways. You're both more open and receptive in the bedroom when there's nothing but you and the night."

"How poetic," Oliver teased, dealing a new hand.

But Charles shifted, unable to hide his very obvious discomfort.

"What's the problem?" Oliver eyed him.

"We…." Shit, he didn't want to admit this.

Both men stopped reviewing their new set of cards and concentrated all of their attention on Charles, staring at him in disbelief. Charles stared out the window between Gideon and George, unable to meet their eyes.

"You're joking," Gideon said in a low voice.

Charles didn't reply.

"Is it her or you or both of you that won't be intimate?" Oliver asked in a voice Charles didn't recognize from his brother.

Again, Charles couldn't bring himself to answer.

"You are a *bastard*," Oliver seethed.

Charles met his younger brother's gaze, the fury completely uncontained on the latter's face.

If Oliver was going to hate him, he may as well hate him properly, Charles thought. Besides, he needed to be upfront in order to get the right guidance on how to fix the mess he made.

"It's more than that," Charles made himself speak. "She tried. On our wedding night, she tried to… but I…."

He didn't know how to complete the thought. He always had the words, the right, appropriate words, yet as always, when it came to the topic of Anna, he had absolutely none.

"Are you telling us," Gideon started, sounding almost dangerous. "Your wife tried to be intimate with you on your wedding night, and you *turned her away?*"

The shame and regret lodged itself in Charles's throat, preventing him from speaking, so he nodded in confirmation.

Gideon turned back to the cards he had spread between his hands with his jaw clenched hard, like he did not even want to look at Charles anymore.

Charles didn't blame him.

"Why?" Oliver demanded.

Charles downed half the amber liquor in his glass before putting it back down and replying, "I don't know."

"Bullshit," Gideon snapped.

"Bullshit," George repeated happily.

Gideon sighed loudly, eyes reaching to the ceiling as he placed his cards face down on the table and turned to his son.

"How is it you know exactly what you're not to say?" Gideon asked him, leaning forward.

George laughed, his eyes sparkling with mischief as he handed one of his cards to his father. Gideon suppressed his smile as he stared with begrudging adoration at the child he was supposed to be scolding. He shook his head before handing the card back like this was George's regular game, and then turned back to the other two men, picking up his cards.

Charles felt a stab of envy watching the interaction between father and son.

"As I was saying," Gideon continued, arranging his cards again. "You do know. If you don't want to tell us, that's your business, but at least be honest with yourself and with your wife. She deserves the truth and to understand, and she deserves a proper husband and marriage."

Charles showed his companions an uncharacteristic expression of his discomfort and stress as he leaned an elbow on the table and rubbed a hand down his face, reaching for his glass again.

"You know she wants children, don't you?" Oliver informed him. "Quite fervently."

Charles's eyes snapped to his brother's. How the hell did he know that? Charles had assumed she probably did. He assumed most women wanted children. How did Oliver know anything about Anna's desire or the strength of it when he, her husband, did not?

"She told Genevieve," Oliver answered without Charles having to ask as the men played their hands. "In the week before the wedding, she told Genevieve she was eager to have children, to watch all of ours grow together, and to have a real, happy marriage with you."

There was a pause as Charles's heart seized in his chest. Fuck, he had ruined things so terribly. Why should she ever reach out to him? He was lucky she didn't spit in his face for trying to talk to her now.

"So, not only did you reject your innocent wife when she was vulnerable," Gideon said, lifting his glass as he leaned back in his chair and driving the point home like a blade. "You shattered both her dreams in one stupid move."

"How do I fix this?" Charles's voice clearly struggled to leave him.

"Step up and be her goddamn husband, you fucking fool," Oliver snapped, grabbing his own tumbler from the table. He clearly had it with his brother.

Charles spun his own tumbler around in circles against the tabletop as his mind spun, berating itself.

"Start courting her," Gideon looped back to their initial suggestion, clearly in a much calmer place than Oliver and able to offer tangible suggestions. "Don't act like things are awkward, even if they are. If you keep acting like it's odd between you, it will continue to be so. And be physical with her. Take it slow if that is what *she* needs, but only then. If it isn't what she needs, and you take your silly little time, it will fuel the rejection she must already be feeling. You need to start putting *her* first."

# CHAPTER 29

## ANNA

"There you are, wife," Charles said in that warm, smooth voice, which was all he ever used with her now, but over the past four days since his visit to Boncroft Hall, there had been a more prominent note of cheerfulness to it. Like he was happy to see her. It amazed her how that small change made her heart feel like it tripled in size.

He strode purposefully into the library towards where she reclined comfortably on the sofa beside the fireplace. The room of wall to wall wood shelves with rolling ladders, broken only by the door, windows, and a fireplace, was her second favorite room in the Manor.

Since adding the large Christmas tree in the entry hall, she and the staff had added the finishing touches to their decorations throughout the Manor, including Charles's study. Wreaths on any remaining empty doors, festive arrangements on any empty tables, garlands along every mantle. She wanted him to have some cheer in his day as he worked.

She had sat down to read her book a little while ago facing the Christmas tree just on the other side of the hearth. The light from the crackling fire made the already warm and comfortable room all the more relaxing as it glinted off the ornaments.

Charles reached her, his light blue eyes sparkling, the edges of his lips hinting at a smile. He bent down, cupping her jaw in his long, artfully masculine hand as he kissed her forehead. Her heart skipped for him in her chest. He'd been doing this more, too, the past few days. Small, tender touches, as if it was the most natural thing in the world. She felt herself already starting to become dependent on them.

Pulling back slightly, he met her eyes again, his thumb stroking her cheek gently. "I've been looking for you," he whispered.

Anna struggled to control her breathing. She wasn't sure what he was doing to her, but her body reacted most enthusiastically to his attentions.

"What do you need?" she whispered.

"What do I need…?" he repeated expectantly.

Anna's lips pulled up in an amused smile. He'd become insistent about this, too. "What do you need, husband?"

"I am glad you asked, wife," he continued seriously, placing a chaste kiss on her lips as if he wasn't trying to stop her heart, and stood up. "Come with me please," he held out his hand.

Closing her book and placing it on the table beside her, she took her husband's hand and returned his smile as she stood.

God, she loved holding his hand. She wanted to go to sleep and wake up every day holding her husband's hand, completely curled around it like she clutched the most precious thing to her heart.

Charles led her from the library, through the Manor, and up the steps of their home. She felt the confusion and amusement mingling in her expression as she wondered what he was doing, but she didn't ask, choosing to simply enjoy the journey.

They reached his bedroom door, and her heart started pounding for a whole new reason.

Was he ready to finally be with her? She was more than ready. With the past week and the strengthening thread that slowly became a proper cord between them, she was ready to make it all the stronger by becoming his wife in truth.

But she didn't want to rush him, either. As she felt herself healing these past days, Anna had also been thinking back on their wedding night with less hurt coloring her vision. To what he said. *I can't.* Not no or that he did not want her. But rather something stopped him, and she realized she had underestimated the depth of his struggles. She was not the only one in this marriage. She was ready, and so, too, did he deserve to be. And Charles was making incredible progress working through those struggles that had kept him apart from her. She would respect his needs and timing.

Opening the door, he pulled her inside her favorite room of her home, and she breathed in the heady scent of the forest that was Charles. It was peculiar how his scent felt like it allowed her to take in a full breath. Like the rest of the time, she could only ever breathe just short of one, but once she inhaled the air marked with him, her lungs could finally fill to the brim.

Her eyes took in the large, warm room. She hadn't been in here since the one and only time she had snuck in. She loved it even more the second time, especially with him standing beside her.

Charles shut the door behind them and let her take in the room. Her eyes immediately zeroed in on what changed. The fire was lit, and the armchairs and table were moved to the side. Spread out on the rug before the fireplace, instead, was a blanket, small pillows, and a basket.

Anna looked up at Charles and found him watching her with the most beautiful, small smile.

"What is this, Charles?" she asked.

He leaned forward and nuzzled her hair, as if he, too,

breathed her in. "A picnic for my wife," he whispered into the strands.

The joy in her chest bubbled up and escaped her in a breathless laugh. She stared at the setup, lifting her free hand to cover her heart.

She looked up and met his still smiling face, his eyes a warm, affectionate baby blue as he looked at her. "Thank you," she said.

He only lifted their joined hands and kissed her knuckles before pulling her forward.

Soon, he had unpacked the basket with their lunch and supplied them both with wine. They were so relaxed, eating and talking and laughing, the romance and sweetness of the gesture erasing everything but this single moment between them.

"So, tell me," Charles said as he reclined, propped up on his elbow. His body faced the fire, legs outstretched, but his head was turned towards her. "When did you come in here?"

Anna was taking a sip of her wine and choked on it before lowering her glass and wiping her lips with her other hand. Charles started laughing at her surprise and lack of composure, head thrown back. He looked so carefree, she forgot about her entirely ruffled reaction at being found out and just drank in the sight of him for full minutes.

He smiled properly, teeth showing, when he looked at her again. She'd never seen this side to him before. Hadn't even realized he possessed it.

"You are ogling me, wife," he observed.

She gave a nervous chuckle before setting her glass down and returning to his question, which was now a safer topic than her attraction to him.

"How did you know?" she asked.

"Because you didn't bother looking around when we came in," he told her. "You looked only at this arrangement as if you recognized it as the change in the room."

She sighed, so comfortable with him now that she let her

honest, inner reactions show. "A few days after the wedding," she admitted.

"And you never told me."

"Because you were so approachable?" she asked with a raised brow.

"Fair point," he agreed, sitting up and reaching for her. He pulled her over to sit between his knees as he wrapped his arms around her.

Anna settled against him, loving the feel of being surrounded by Charles. This was her favorite place in all the world, she realized, here in her husband's arms. She leaned her head against his shoulder as they stared into the fire.

After a moment, she asked, "You aren't upset?"

"By what?" He looked down at her face. "By you coming in here? Not at all. This is your home, Anna. You own each and every room within it. And soon, this will be your room, too." He kissed the top of her head sweetly.

"Will it?" Her heart began to race a little with excitement. Could he mean that? She wanted it so badly.

"Of course," he said, voice low and sincere. "Or if you prefer yours, I could move myself there. It does not matter to me which room we use, so long as we share one."

Her chest felt like it would split open, it felt so full. She wasn't sure she could get the words out. "This one," she managed to whisper.

He gave her that small, warm smile again that she was falling in love with. "Then this one it shall be, wife."

They sat in comfortable silence for a little longer, Charles resting his head atop hers as they watched the flames.

"Charles?"

"Yes?"

"Do you recall the night of our family dinner? What you said to me?"

"I believe I said many things," Charles replied expectantly.

Anna pulled in a breath. If she wanted to know, she would have to ask properly and not let her nerves overrun her.

She instilled confidence into her voice as she clarified, "You told me you were mine. That you have never been, nor will you ever be, anyone else's. Is that true?"

"Of course, it's true," his brow furrowed. He was getting comfortable with her, too. Showing his reactions through his expression, smiles, laughter. He was letting her in.

"You have never been with anyone else?" she finally asked directly, getting to the heart of her question. The question that had niggled at the back of her mind since he'd said it. Her curiosity growing with each passing day and step closer between them.

Finally, Charles understood, and his face cleared of its confusion, shifting instead to amusement. She loved how he let her read his thoughts on his face now.

"Why, wife, are you asking if I'm a virgin?" he teased. She felt his chest vibrating behind her as he chuckled.

She also loved every time he laughed. She loved so many things about him.

"Yes," she replied honestly, holding his gaze. Now that the question was asked, she would not feel embarrassed by it.

"Of course, I am," he told her, still chortling with amusement.

She could not believe it. "Truly?"

"Truly," he nodded, eyes smiling.

"I don't believe it," she voiced the thought out loud.

"You wound me, wife," he feigned offense, but then his gaze turned serious. "Did you really think I would not be faithful to you, Anna?"

"I...," she paused, considering. "Truthfully, I did not know. But even if you planned to be once we were married, I had not expected it before we were wed."

"Were you faithful to me before our wedding?" he asked.

"Of course," she replied immediately and a little indignantly.
"Why?"

"Because you are my husband."

"Why is it then so hard to believe I would be faithful to you?"
he replied softly, his deep voice pouring over her with honesty
and insight into his heart and mind. "You have been my wife
since I was ten, Anna. Our vows simply allowed me to bring you
home."

# CHAPTER 30

## CHARLES

*C*harles stared at his wife's shocked face. She was still processing that, even though she'd been committed and faithful to him her entire life, he had also paid her the same respect. His eyes traced the freckles across the bridge of her nose as she absorbed his words.

"I...," she started, and Charles's heart beat hopefully for the three words he was desperate to hear but also terrified of sharing with her.

He was trying to be a better man and husband, but he hadn't defeated his cowardice enough to admit it to her yet.

She shook her head, and his chest deflated the tiniest bit. They were still making leaps and bounds in their relationship, even with the way she shook her head. They were both letting their small gestures out with each other. Things they did not show others. And she'd been receptive to sharing a room with him when they were ready. They would get there with their words, too.

Then, Anna sat up from where she leaned against his chest. He loved holding her. It felt like they belonged like that, holding each other. She fit so perfectly against him.

She turned to him with determination and placed her lips on his. The kiss was sweet, and it brought him peace understanding that it likely always would be, and it immediately ignited the fire in his blood.

The closer they became, the more his body craved hers.

She rested one hand on his chest, while the other snaked up his shoulder and neck to tangle in his hair. He pulled her close, but their position prevented him from having her flush against him as he wanted.

Her tongue darted out, seeking his, and he angled his head, deepening the kiss to coax and match her tender strokes. God, he loved kissing her. He loved everything about her. There wasn't a damned thing he did not love.

He couldn't take it. His cock strained against his clothing as he grabbed her legs, urging her to straddle him.

She reacted immediately, turning fully and pulling up her dress enough so she could get as close as they both needed, wrapping her arms around his shoulders.

He couldn't stop his hands from sliding up her legs, pushing her skirts up further as his hands moved under them. He dislodged them enough that he could feel the heat of her arousal against his hardness. The groan that left him was unlike any sound he'd ever made in his life.

Their kiss grew more frenzied. Still sweet, still tender, but also edging closer and closer towards mindless.

Then his wife arched against his cock, giving them both the friction they ached for, and pleasure rocketed through him. It must have had a similar effect on her because she pulled her lips from his with a moan. Without missing a beat, he dropped his head and began kissing down her neck, desperate to keep the taste of her on his tongue. Anna angled her head to give him better access, her delicate pants like music to his ears. His hips bucked instinctively, seeking her heat, and her fingers holding onto his hair tightened.

Charles found the ties at the back of dress and pulled, untying her dress before pushing it down to gather at her waist. She released his hair to undo his cravat, vest, and shirt, while he worked on her stays. Then, he pulled her chemise down to her waist, as well, while she pushed all his layers of clothing off his shoulders.

For a full minute, they both just explored each other, fingertips trailing over one another's skin, gently, softly, adoringly. She traced the shape of his shoulders, ran down his chest, splayed her fingers through the hair there, while he trailed his hands up her stomach, along the curve of her breast, around her pebbled nipple. She shivered, breaking the spell, and they met each other's eyes for a moment before he cupped both breasts more firmly. He rubbed the pads of his thumbs over her hardened nipples and watched her reaction with rapture as she closed her eyes and bit her exquisitely full bottom lip, a soft groan escaping her.

Charles shifted then, urging her to stand while he sat up onto his knees. She did, and her eyes went straight to the outline of his length as her clothes finally fell to the floor, pooling at her feet. He removed the last of her undergarments, leaving her naked before him. She started to reach down to touch him, but he caught her hand and kissed her palm.

"Lay back, wife," he gestured with his other hand for her to lie before the fire. "There is something I would like to try."

Anna met his eyes before obliging. She laid down on the blanket, propping herself up on her elbows as she watched him with expectation and trust.

Charles couldn't breathe for a moment as he looked at her. She stunned him, his wife. Her unusual, otherworldly beauty. Her pale, soft skin. Her sweet, humble curves. And *trust*.

He grabbed one of the small pillows to place behind her before he moved to hover over her, settling his hips between her parted thighs. He could sense her nervousness, mirroring his own.

"You are the most beautiful thing in my world, Anna Sinclair," he told his wife truthfully, loving the sound of her full name. Then, he kissed her, and she relaxed fully at the feel of his words and his lips.

Ignoring his anxiety and pounding heart, Charles broke the kiss and began to move down her body, kissing her neck, her breasts, taking each nipple into his mouth before he made his way down to his intended destination.

Anna only made small noises of arousal, but he could feel her tension increase as he passed below her belly button. When he reached her center, he pushed her legs further apart, hoping he did this right, and looked at her. She was pink and wet for him, and his body ached with the desperate desire to be inside her. But not today.

"Tell me what feels good," he said, voice low and rough, and before he could second guess himself, he licked along her seam.

Her taste erupted along his tongue, beyond anything he could have ever imagined. And it must have felt good for her, too, because her hips immediately lifted, pushing further against his mouth. He wrapped his hands around her thighs and pulled her against him as he continued to stroke her cautiously for a bit. When he finally plunged his tongue inside her, she moaned loudly.

"Yes, Charles," she panted, and he looked up to see her head tilted back, eyes closed as she found her pleasure. "*Yes.*" She seemed unable to string proper words together, and he took that as yet more confirmation that he was doing well.

Anna took hold of his hand, clutching his fingers tightly. He kept fucking her with his tongue for another moment before he moved up to her clit, unwrapping his other hand from her thigh to stroke inside her with his finger instead.

Her grip on his hand became almost painful, words abandoning her completely at the shift in his approach. He flicked his tongue against her, pulling the loudest moan from her yet. His confidence having grown with her responses, Charles suddenly wanted to see if he could make her scream from his ministrations. So, he flicked his tongue again, harder and faster, and added another finger inside her.

Anna tensed around him, her body starting to tremble. He continued working her over, her shaking growing in intensity as he did so. And then he tried biting her ever so slightly between flicks, and his wife came apart with a scream, clenching around him.

Charles kept his fingers moving inside her, his tongue against her until he felt her go lax and her hand release him. Then, he pulled his mouth from her and looked up.

She was absolutely breathtaking. Her face flushed, chest moving rapidly up and down as she panted, her other hand now loose over the wrinkled picnic blanket she must have been clutching along with his fingers.

He kissed her inner thigh before removing his body from hers and sitting back on his knees. She opened her eyes to look at him, the blue crystals glazed and hooded, and his already painfully hard cock pulsed further.

"May I give you the same, husband?" his wife asked in such a sultry voice, she could have probably made him come just by demanding it.

# CHAPTER 31

## ANNA

*A*nna was still floating down to Earth, but she had never felt more alive. Every nerve, every inch of her skin was alive in a way she'd never been before or even known was possible.

He'd made her feel so amazing, and now, she wanted to do the same for him.

Before he could respond, she sat up and began undoing his breeches.

Charles didn't say anything, but after a moment's hesitation, he helped her. Then, she freed him from his clothing. His cock sprang forth as if eager for her, and Anna licked her lips at the sight of him. He was already beautiful, every part of him she'd seen. His face, his shoulders, his chest, his arms. Everything about him was so refined, so strong, so *male*, just the sight had her body turning molten and heat gathering between her legs. His cock was no less masculine and beautiful. She grasped the base of it with one hand, surprised by the softness of his skin.

"Stand up, husband," she lifted her eyes to meet his, and the hunger burning in his made her feel so powerfully feminine, she relished the feeling.

He did as instructed, and she released him to spin her legs around and get on her knees, pushing his clothes off him completely.

She looked up at him again, his eyes still watching her silently. She noticed something more delicate in his gaze, too, and Anna was overwhelmed by the sense that, while she was on her knees, Charles was really the one in worship.

With that thought, she gathered her courage and took the tip of him into her mouth, circling her tongue gently around him as she learned the taste and shape of him. Charles groaned so powerfully, heat gathered between her legs once more at the sheer *maleness* of the sound. His hand was at the back of her head, holding her gently as she tried to relax her jaw and let more of him in.

He was too large to fit all the way, but she began to gently stroke him with her mouth, sensing his pleasure by his low groans and the change in his breathing. The hand behind her head stayed loose, as if simply holding her. She began to move her hand in tandem with her mouth, trying to stroke him fully.

"Firmer, wife," his voice could have been a growl, it was so deep and rough.

She was only too happy to oblige, tightening both her hand and her lips around him. His rewarding sound was so erotic, her own arousal multiplied as if she hadn't already finished at all. She began to explore his body with her other hand, which had been resting on his thigh. She moved it up and down his leg slowly before reaching up to stroke his stomach. When she reached down to explore his sack, Charles gripped her hair tightly. She read the pleasure in the action and kept her hand there, touching him softly.

He was losing control, the hand now clutching her hair starting to gently guide her pace, and she appreciated the insight into what felt good for him. She tried hollowing her cheeks to see if he liked that, and his groans grew in intensity.

And when she finally pressed her tongue against him, he came so forcefully, she froze with her initial shock. Then, she moved slowly, matching his continued movements and swallowing down his seed as she pumped the last of it into her mouth.

When his hold loosened on her hair, she pulled back and smiled up at him. She felt like the most formidable woman in the world to have given him so much pleasure. To have made her strong, endlessly composed husband lose his control. She knew this wasn't the full act of sex, but she already loved every part they'd just experienced. And giving him pleasure had aroused her so acutely, she needed more.

But it was the way he blinked down at her, his hand shifting from the back of her head to cup her jaw. He traced her bottom lip with his thumb before he bent down and grabbed both of her shoulders, urging her to stand.

She did, and once she was fully upright, he wrapped his arms tightly around her and simply held her to him. Her arms encircled his waist on instinct, and she rested her head against his chest. They stayed like that for several minutes. Perfectly content and whole, hearts beating together with their every happiness and hope.

Neither one of them spoke. They did not need to.

# CHAPTER 32

## CHARLES

*C*harles crossed his bedroom towards the door to the hall, glancing at the chairs and table now back in their proper place before the fireplace as he did. The smile had yet to leave his face since he and his wife had their indoor picnic two days ago. And since that day, the comfort and easy, familiar intimacy between them had Charles impatient to see her any time they were apart.

After they'd simply held each other that day, silent and accepting, they had gotten dressed. Anna left for her bedroom to compose herself, while Charles packed up the remnants of their lunch. He didn't want to finish things between them yet and continue to the bed. The day had been perfect, and he didn't want to ruin it by pushing too fast too soon. It had been months, years that they had been distant with each other. He wanted to do things perfectly now, make their marriage and their relationship as stable as possible, so when they finally did make love, there would be no doubt, wariness, hesitation between them.

Now, it was time for them to entertain. Christmas was five days away, and their final few guests, including Anna's parents, were expected to arrive over the next three days. Their close friends, however, had arrived yesterday, and tonight was their first dinner party. The first of many, Charles thought happily, that he and his wife would host for them. Thomas and Lydia were staying with Gideon and Amelia; Philip and Alexander were at Boncroft Hall; and the Davenport siblings were set up in Sinclair Manor.

Charles had a spring in his step as he entered the hallway. Then, he spotted his wife a few paces down the hall, her dark blue dress hugging her petite figure deliciously as it swayed with each step. Charles shut his door quickly and quietly before hurrying after her with light footsteps she wouldn't hear. He was on her in a moment, grabbing her gloved hand. She gave a surprised yelp as he pulled her into the nearest room, which he was glad remained unoccupied by any guest.

The room was dark and cold as he stepped through, shutting the door behind his now giggling wife. *Giggling.* Heavens, they were so unlike the versions of themselves from the past nearly two decades.

To further the point, Charles had Anna pushed up against the door not a second later.

Since they'd shared some intimacies together two days ago, their kisses had become far more passionate. They were still soft, still sweet, like his sweet, amazing wife, but a hunger brewed there now that was fast becoming ravenous, desperate.

He kissed her like a man completely and utterly under her spell, because he was. He wanted her. He wanted his mouth on every inch of her again. He wanted hers on every inch of him. Charles had barely started kissing her when they were already frenzied, and she moaned in that sweet, delectable way that drove him mad. His cock rose to the occasion not a heartbeat later.

Anna wrapped her arms around his shoulders and pulled at him as though she could not get him close enough. And he understood. He had one hand at her hip, pulling her against his straining length, the other cupping and squeezing her breast through the silk of her dress, wishing he could feel her skin against his instead.

Anna pulled her mouth from his, but he just shifted to kiss the edge of her jaw and lick his way down her neck. He was growing more confident, too, being physical with her.

"Husband," she said in a breathy voice that had a pleased rumble moving through his chest. She moaned again, her head tilting to expose more of her neck.

"Charles," she tried again. "Our guests are waiting."

"Let them wait, wife," his voice vibrated against her shoulder as he kissed across her collarbone. "I have more pressing needs."

"Do you?" she asked on another moan. God, her moans and the easy way with which she bestowed them were addicting. "What needs are those?"

"I need you," he whispered honestly.

"Then, *take me*, husband," she said in a low, raspy voice. "Please, *please* take me."

The words hit him like a bolt of lightning. He knew she wanted him, too. That it wasn't just Charles who ached to finally, *finally* have him buried deep inside her, and when she begged to have exactly that, it was damn near impossible to remember that he wanted to wait.

He groaned like it physically pained him, which it absolutely did, as he moved back to her mouth, kissing her one last time before he pulled away, putting a step of distance between them.

Her chest rose and fell on rapid breaths, and her gaze was hooded, but he was still close enough to recognize the confusion in her eyes at his retreat.

"Soon," he vowed, reaching a hand out to cup her stunning face. She closed her eyes and leaned into him, and his heart swelled. He loved that they could have their passion while the tender, gentle connection between them remained resolutely in place. The core of who they were. "I promise we'll be together soon."

She assessed him a moment longer, then reached up to circle his wrist with her small fingers. She turned her face into his palm and kissed it. His skin tingled at the contact.

"Alright," she replied before lowering his hand from her face and wrapping hers around his other arm instead. She gave him that small smile of hers and gestured to the door. "Shall we?"

Charles kissed her forehead before opening it and escorting his wife to dinner.

# CHAPTER 33

## ANNA

*A*nna was far too aroused as she and Charles made their way to the drawing room. Her blood was hot as it pumped through her, her skin tight and needy for his touch, her core wet and ready for him.

But Charles still was not ready. Even after the other day, that wonderful, amazing picnic he'd set up for her in his bedroom. The room he said they'd one day share, but did not specify when. Or everything that happened after they'd eaten. The pleasure they'd found with one another. She thought they would finally make love then, or at least that night, but they didn't. She was too relaxed, happy, sated at the time to mind too much, but the passion had clearly increased between them drastically since then, and it was getting harder for her to keep her hands to herself. To wait until he was ready. She wasn't sure what continued to hold him back, and she did not want to push too hard, but she couldn't stop the confusion and doubt forming in the recesses of her mind. Not to mention her body's growing demands these past few days with every kiss, every touch, even every look.

They stepped into their drawing room to find everyone

already gathered, which she'd anticipated given the surprise delay Charles had maneuvered upstairs. Oliver, Genevieve, Gideon, Amelia, Thomas, Lydia, Philip, Alexander, Jack, Emily, and Grace were spread loosely throughout the spacious room, engaged in various conversations. As soon as their hosts entered, however, their discussions came to an abrupt halt. Neither Anna nor Charles gave any indication that they noticed the silence or the way their friends' eyes followed them as they crossed the room, but she noted their mixture of surprise, smirks, and bemusement. It seemed none of them expected to finally see the newfound ease between Charles and Anna.

They broke apart to greet their guests, and Anna eventually seated herself on the armchair farthest from the blazing fire. The last thing she needed was more heat near her already over-heated body.

"How are Adelaide and John?" Anna asked Lydia, who sat nearest her on the sofa with Amelia and Grace.

"Perfectly happy and up to their usual mischief with their cousins," Lydia told her in that lovely soothing voice of hers before shifting the conversation to what was on her mind. "But the Manor looks wonderful, Anna. You have done such a splendid job with it."

"It's so festive," Emily added brightly from the couch opposite, seated beside Genevieve. Anna was so happy to see her, and she hoped they would get some time alone together soon. She hadn't realized how deeply she missed her friend until she was right in front of her again.

"Practically brimming with cheer," Philip replied, seeming to finish her thought from where he stood beside Alexander and Jack, eyes sparkling with mischief as he looked at Emily.

"Practically?" Emily continued, not missing a beat. "Over-whelmingly, you mean."

"Is it too much?" Anna asked, not really self-conscious but

still tossing a critical eye around the Christmas arrangements, the garland and wreaths, the tree artfully decorating the room.

"It's perfect," Charles answered, speaking from beside the mantelpiece, where she had assumed he was engaged in a more intimate discussion with Oliver, Gideon, and Thomas. They must have refocused their attentions to the larger group, although Charles's seemed quite singularly focused on her alone.

"Quite," Amelia agreed. Anna's gaze flicked across the ladies to find them all wearing varying degrees of satisfied smiles. Oliver clapped Charles on the shoulder, muttering something.

"The more cheerful the better, I say," Emily beamed.

"You haven't done much redecorating," Genevieve observed. "Are you waiting until after the holidays?"

"Yes, as long as Charles does not mind," Anna nodded towards her husband. "There are several changes I have considered these past weeks."

"Why should I mind?" Charles asked. "It's *your* house."

"It's yours, too," Anna countered.

"What do I care about wallpaper and furniture?"

"For the love of God, please fix the dining room," Oliver pleaded. "I hate that orange wallpaper —."

"I always thought it more red than orange," Genevieve interrupted thoughtfully.

"Whatever it is, it's horrendous," Oliver finished.

"It's not that awful," Gideon offered.

"It's a bit awful," Thomas said apologetically.

"I have a few ideas for some of rooms," Emily added with her natural enthusiasm.

"When did you see their rooms?" Philip asked her.

"During the wedding, which *you* missed, My Lord," she winked, addressing him with a teasing sarcasm.

"My Mother was unable to travel." The way he spoke seemed to address Emily alone. It was uncanny how quickly the interaction between the two of them seemed to shift from a group dynamic to an easy, private familiarity that only they two shared. "And I hesitated to leave her twice in a single month."

Concern etched itself into Emily's features, and Anna's eyes moved between the two of them. She realized there was a much deeper comfort there than she had previously noticed. Now that she did, it was incredibly obvious. Anna had seen how Philip and Emily often paired off last Season as their group socialized, but it seemed a real, personal friendship had grown between the two.

"It is up to my wife," Charles said, closing the argument and pulling Anna's attention away from her best friend and the viscount. Those light blue eyes watched her with so much focus and affection as he continued, "Whatever she wants, however she wants it, that is what we shall do."

Anna didn't bother trying to hide or subdue the full smile that broke across her face as she looked at her husband. His answering smirk set her heart fluttering.

When dinner was finally called, however, she did not get to walk with her husband to the dining room as she wanted. Genevieve and Emily swooped in rather quickly to walk arm in arm with her instead, trapping her between them.

"Things seem to have gotten much better," Genevieve whispered so only she and Emily could hear as they walked, the hope and question ringing loudly in the words.

"They have," Anna replied, a smile pulling at her lips.

"Thank goodness," Emily spoke in an uncharacteristically low and relieved voice. "I was dreadfully worried after the wedding and Genevieve's letter."

Anna scowled at her sister-in-law.

"Don't look at me like that," Genevieve said, completely unapologetic. "We were concerned."

"Is everything truly okay now, Anna?" Emily asked, her sunny friend's voice serious.

Anna hesitated, the niggling doubt in the back of her mind that she tried to ignore preventing her from lying outright. But she also didn't want to share with them that she and Charles had yet to be fully intimate together. She just didn't know why her husband, who was clearly trying to build a proper marriage with her, still refused to share her bed.

"We are getting there," she finally replied as they reached the brightly lit dining room, beautiful and extravagant for their first formal dinner party, even with the rather unsavory wallpaper that she intended to change first in her redecorating.

The rest of the night passed with such happiness and joy, Anna could scarcely remember a better one. The twinkling candlelight, the delicious food, the warm atmosphere, and the love and friendship around their fine table filled her soul as they all talked, laughed, and ate.

# CHAPTER 34

## CHARLES

*C*hristmas Eve. His first Christmas with his wife, and their first Christmas Ball at Sinclair Manor together. Charles was in such a wonderful place. Truth be told, he'd been soaring since that day in his bedroom, and he had yet to come down. His brother and friends had been pleased seeing the progress between him and his wife at dinner four nights ago. Oliver, Gideon, and Thomas immediately asked after their relationship and expressed their immense relief before dinner had even started.

Charles approached the closed dark wooden door between his bedroom and his wife's, hesitating. He had never approached this door without prompting – the one and only time had been when he answered her knock on their wedding night. Now, dressed in his Christmas finery, he was unsure if he should knock or just open it.

No, he was erasing the walls between them. This was an opportunity to eradicate yet another. So, he grabbed the gold doorknob with forced confidence and opened the barrier between them.

Anna sat at her dressing table across the room, her maid,

Elsie, standing behind her as she pinned jewels into his wife's lovely red locks. Her eyes found his in her reflection, but Charles stood frozen in the doorway.

Anna's lips pulled up, her crystal blue eyes sparkling with amusement and pleasure at seeing him stuck in the doorway between their rooms. Charles shook off his stupor. Stepping properly into the room, he became aware of Elsie's face shifting from an expression of shock to pleasure. She finished adding the final pin into Anna's perfectly coiffed hair and then excused herself.

Charles still did not speak as she stood, picking up her gloves from the dressing table, and turned to him. His eyes drank her in, tracing down her body and then back up. She was poised and elegant in her rich burgundy silk, the embellished dress hugging her body both tastefully and seductively.

"Well, this is a pleasant surprise," she breathed as she took a step in his direction. Charles finally snapped to his senses and bridged the gap between them with quick strides.

He couldn't find the words. Even with all their progress, that still had not changed. How Anna always robbed Charles of his words, he did not know, but his hand cupped her face, his eyes counting the overabundance of freckles he loved so much. He trailed his fingers down her neck, across her collarbone, his touch light and reverent. Then, he moved along the edge of her neckline and across the sweet swell of her breasts, which started to strain against the fabric to accommodate her increased breathing. Goosebumps followed in the wake of his touch, mesmerizing him.

He lifted his eyes to find her gaze hooded, the slightest part to her sultry lips.

"You are so beautiful," he said in a low, awed voice.

He watched her throat work on a swallow, marveling at the beauty of her and every gesture she shared with him.

"Shall we?" he asked in the same voice, finally removing his hand from where her skin burned his with their combined, potent desire, and held out his arm.

Anna made quick work of putting on her gloves and then wrapped her hand around him. Slightly more composed, she spoke as he led her to the bedroom door, "You are rather beautiful yourself, Charles."

Pleasure bloomed within him at the compliment as he shut the door behind them and smirked down at her. "Am I, indeed?"

She only nodded, serious and regal as they walked towards the staircase that would lead them to their party. "You have always been the handsomest man I've ever known."

"I hope that never changes," he told her honestly.

"It won't," she promised.

SINCLAIR MANOR WAS alive in a way Charles could not remember it being before. His mother's balls had never been dull or lacking, but to see his wife's hand painting his home was a dream. The whole Manor was lit and animated with Christmas cheer, the rooms bright, the trees and decorations sparkling as he passed by them towards the ballroom. Yet still, he hadn't been prepared for the lavish center of tonight's party. The ballroom glittered. Tables topped with large Christmas arrangements and towers of refreshments and eggnog. A large tree almost as big as the proud pine in the entryway held centerstage on the dancefloor, the light of the chandeliers glinting off its many ornaments. Their guests already danced to the joyful music. Eating, drinking, and laughing, the cheer of the room contagious. The room even smelled of Christmas with pine and spice assaulting his nose in the most pleasant of ways as soon as they entered.

"Anna," he breathed as he stopped them to the side of the large double doors, his voice shocked as his eyes continued to find more glittering gold, warm green, bright red as he took in the room.

"Do you like it?" she asked, her voice nervous.

"I love it," he answered, looking down at her. "You astonish me, Anna. Whenever I think I could not be prouder to have you as my wife, you prove me wrong again and again."

Anna, his warm, stoic wife, *blushed*. She never blushed, and Charles didn't care how improper it was or who he embarrassed as he lifted his free hand to her face and kissed her. It was short and sweet, but his lips tingled and heated at the quick touch.

He wanted to say it. To tell her. But he didn't want to profess his heart to her in a room surrounded by others.

So, instead, he said, "You owe me a dance, wife."

"I do not recall making such a promise," she quipped, and he was thrilled at this teasing, fun side to her that she had opened up to him.

"You made it the day you married me."

Her lips squeezed together, the natural tilt still pulling them up as she fought her amusement while Charles led them onto the dancefloor.

"Perhaps I missed that part of our wedding vows," she replied when he pulled her into his arms, his body achingly aware and craving hers. She furrowed her brow in mock concentration as she pretended to remember their vows.

God, the mischief in her eyes. How could he have gone eighteen years keeping himself away from that? From her?

"Then you weren't paying close enough attention," he spun her around the dancefloor, the music, the fragrance, the magic, his feelings overtaking him. "All your dances and smiles. Your nights and mornings. All your days, wife, and all your dreams. You owe them to me, and you have all of mine in return."

# CHAPTER 35

## ANNA

*A*nna finally made it over to one of her towering refreshment tables and picked up a glass of eggnog. Taking a sip of the sweet, creamy beverage, she looked around at the bustling ballroom. Her parents and mother-in-law socialized with some of the older family guests that had known the Sinclairs for years. Genevieve, Amelia, and Grace conversed happily as they strolled along the edge of the room. Thomas and Lydia were dancing, as were Philip and Emily. And Charles was actually smiling publicly as he enjoyed an exchange with Oliver, Gideon, Alexander, and Jack.

Heavens, she could not remember a more magical night.

She would have kept staring at her husband had her curiosity not pulled her back towards the dancefloor. Philip and Emily had piqued her interest the other night. The familiarity between the two of them. Taking another sip of her eggnog, she considered them. Emily was as bright and sparkling as the room in all its holiday glory, and she and Philip danced as if they had grown familiar to the way the other moved, which wasn't surprising given how often they paired off. The more she watched, Anna had to admit that Philip wasn't looking at her like a man in love, neither did Emily seem exceptionally besotted with him, but still, there was a noticeable... ease between them. They talked as they moved, spinning around the dancefloor.

Anna tilted her head and wondered, holding the crystal lightly in her hand. She had always imagined that if anyone's love story would be made of fireworks and crackling love, it would be Emily's. She was a firework in and of herself. But now that Anna watched them, she wondered if she had been mistaken. Maybe her friend's romance wouldn't be a flash of bright, passionate light, but the soft, steady calmness of the night.

The song ended, and Emily caught her eye. Excusing herself, her best friend made her way to Anna still standing by the table of towering crystal and holly.

"What are you staring at?" Emily asked, picking up a glass of eggnog and coming around to stand beside Anna, her dark green dress swishing.

"Nothing," Anna said, keeping her thoughts to herself. She took another sip of her drink just as Emily did, licking her lips before she asked, "How are you enjoying the evening? I think everything came together quite splendidly."

"Of course, it did," Emily said vibrantly. "I'm having a wonderful time. I think you and Charles should hold every Christmas Ball from now on."

Anna chuckled. "We might just." Trying to seem casual, she observed, "You and Philip seem to have become rather good friends."

"We have," Emily nodded, glancing over at the viscount, who had joined the men by the window. "He's a delightful man."

"Who is?" Genevieve asked coming up beside them on Emily's other side. Anna hadn't noticed her approach, even with the bright red dress she wore.

"Philip," Anna told her sister-in-law.

"Yes," Genevieve glanced surreptitiously at Emily. Good, it seemed Genevieve had cottoned on to the same thing Anna had. Together, they could perhaps work on bringing Emily and Philip closer. "Delightful, and incredibly sweet."

"How is the readying for motherhood going, Genevieve?" Emily asked.

Genevieve's hand went subconsciously to her stomach as she answered, "Quite well." She smiled so contentedly that Anna was struck with equal parts joy for her sister-in-law and envy. "Although, Mother and Amelia stitched the most ridiculous blanket for the baby, and I don't have the heart to tell them we can never actually use it."

"What's wrong with it?" Anna asked.

"Oh, nothing is *wrong* with it," Genevieve replied, eyeing one of the cakes on the table before picking it up. "It's absolutely gorgeous with their truly intricate stitching, but it is completely useless. I'm surprised both of them being mothers, and Amelia expecting her third now, would think any child could sleep under such a thing."

"Perhaps they meant it more decoratively," Anna suggested.

"I thought so, too, until I tried to put it on display in the nursery rather than on the bed. They both reacted quite passionately. Mother practically tore it from my hand and moved it to the bed, while Amelia looked ready to cry. I expect that's because of the baby, though. I find myself close to tears quite often, too."

Anna and Emily were both laughing by the time Genevieve finished speaking, and she joined in, chuckling and shaking her head as she ate her cake.

"You'll just have to use a proper blanket and then remember to bring it out whenever they visit," Emily told her.

"Mother is living with us," Genevieve reminded her after swallowing her bite.

"Well, then, let her see how impractical it is once the baby fusses," Emily replied.

"That is likely what we will have to do," Genevieve agreed, taking another bite.

Anna smiled and decided she needed a little breather. Finishing the last of her eggnog, she told her friends she would be back shortly and made her way across the ballroom to the doors leading to the hallway. She handed off her glass to a passing footman with a smile and word of thanks.

As soon as she left the ballroom, she enjoyed the immediate reprieve, greeting a few of the guests who had a similar mind and mingled in the quieter hallway. She kept walking, making her way to the empty entry hall and crossing to the staircase. She planned to only take a few minutes of solitude in her bedroom, check her appearance, and return.

She was more than halfway up the staircase when a voice stopped her, making her spine stiffen and heart stop.

"My dear Anna," the overfamiliar voice drawled, and she turned to find Geoffrey Perkins climbing the steps behind her.

Her heart started again, racing with trepidation. This man had followed her. She knew it immediately.

Truthfully, Anna had forgotten about Geoffrey Perkins this past week and a half. She'd been so caught up in things with Charles that the steward had fallen from her mind completely, and now she cursed her own lack of foresight. She should have spoken to Charles, whether things were difficult between them or not.

Because Geoffrey Perkins was not following Anna with any sort of positive intent.

She clutched her skirts as her eyes bounced between monitoring his approach and searching the empty entry hall for any passing help. She did not know how she would get away from him. Her only open path lay behind her, further up the stairs, and that presented even more danger.

"Where are you running off to, you lovely creature," his smile was sharp, and she did not like the triumph glinting in his eyes as they trailed down to her feet and back up. How long had he been waiting to get her alone? He hadn't been in the ball-room, she would have noticed. Had he been waiting out here, hoping to trap her alone?

He was four steps away from her now. If she tried to dodge around him and go back down the way she'd come, she had the very strong sense that he would grab for her.

Her only choice was to stand her ground and try to bully him away.

She pulled her shoulders back and demanded, "What the hell do you think you're doing, Mr. Perkins?"

He came to a stop on the step below hers, one foot resting next to her. Panic was a living, clawing thing within her as she realized what he did. He had caged her in. She hoped he couldn't see how her hands trembled where she clutched her dress. She needed to intimidate him away from her.

"My, my," he leered, and she tried not to show how her body recoiled. She could not show weakness. "What language, Anna. I thought you were the 'Lady of the Manor.' Those aren't the words of a lady, nor the hospitality of one."

"Sir, you forget yourself," she kept her voice firm, focusing on her anger and hiding her fear. "You will address me as Mrs. Sinclair, and I demand that you return to the ball immediately. You may not follow me."

"Oh, I saw you, *Mrs. Sinclair*," the steward sneered as his gaze dropped to her lips. Her panic grew drastically. He lifted his hand and grasped her chin between his thumb and forefinger, and the shock that he would cross the physical barrier made her terror crippling. She froze on the spot. "It seems you and your husband are quite familiar yourselves now with how he kissed you in front of everyone. What a shame. I thought I might get to seduce you first."

Anna reacted on pure instinct, no longer caring if her fear showed or not. "Get your hands off me," she almost screamed, her voice high as she smacked his arm away and ran two steps up with an uncontrollable instinct to flee. She didn't have to wonder at her next move though, thankfully, as the steward was yanked backwards and thrown tumbling down the stairs while she made her retreat.

Charles stood on the staircase, and the relief that poured through Anna almost made her sob. He looked like a vengeful angel, full of wrath and fury as he stared down to where he'd thrown Geoffrey Perkins with dangerous stillness.

He moved, each step down the staircase slow and deliberate, but as the fear drained out of her, leaving a shaking chill in its wake, she noticed how Charles's chest rose and fell on deep, measured breaths. He was *furious*.

"Do you think," Charles's voice was even, cold, deadly, "you can touch my wife?" He kept descending the stairs. "That you can come into our home, lay your filthy little finger on her, and I would *let you*?" Charles reached the foot of the stairs and stood over the now scared looking man, who had gotten to his feet and clearly knew he didn't stand a chance on his best day against Charles Sinclair.

"You misunderstand –," the steward started in a weak voice.

Charles's fist shot out before Anna could even blink. The steward flew backwards, landing on the ground before he turned back around, hand going to his bleeding and likely broken nose, as he watched Charles approach him again.

"I didn't mean –," he said, the terror breaking his voice.

*Good*, Anna thought where she still stood fixed on the stairs. Let *him* be the one terrified.

Charles grabbed the steward by his coat, lifting him up and slamming him against the wall.

"If you ever come near my wife again," Charles spoke. "I will kill you." He delivered the words with such contained, calm rage, his voice absolutely lethal, that Anna felt chills run uncomfortably down her spine.

She believed him.

With that, he tossed the man one last time towards the door, where Smith now stood, looking down at the steward with utter disgust and anger on his face.

Anna's attention now went to the rest of the entry hall, realizing the commotion had dragged their guests out of the ballroom. But as she watched, still on the stairs, leaning back with relief against the wall, she noticed their loved ones handling the situation. Oliver, Gideon, Thomas, and Alexander were more than halfway across the entry hall, looks of fury on their faces as they handled Geoffrey Perkins the rest of the way out with Smith. Philip, Jack, Genevieve, and Amelia were ushering the last of their guests back towards the ballroom, while her mother-in-law, parents, Lydia, Emily, and Grace placed themselves throughout the crowd and seemed to be managing and shifting the conversation as they led the retreat.

And then Charles was right in front of her, blocking off her view of everything going on below.

"*Anna.*" He said her name with such concern and care, his hand cradling her face as he peered at her with worry etched into his features and drowning his baby blue eyes.

She leaned her head into his hand, her eyes closing. Feeling his touch, breathing his scent, hearing his voice, the fear and relief finally escaped her in a choked sob.

# CHAPTER 36

## CHARLES

"You both should go now," Oliver said quietly to Charles where they stood at the edge of the dance-floor. They had rejoined the party for the past few hours, and Charles refused to let Anna out of his sight. He'd been aware of her all night and had watched her leave the ballroom earlier. Not wanting to miss an opportunity to be alone with his wife, he had excused himself as soon as he was able and followed her.

That's when he came upon that rat cornering her on the staircase. Everything else had left Charles's mind in that moment except for a cold, unending rage.

Since then, they'd returned to the ballroom once Anna felt ready and the evening had picked back up. Their close friends were so many and so thorough that they had seamlessly moved the rest of the guests past any drama or attempts at gossip and brought the evening back to its original festivities.

But Charles had watched his wife as he did his part. She was flawless. Smiling warmly, mingling, talking, but he saw the tension in her eyes, the way she carried herself, how the smile never quite moved beyond the slight pull of her lips.

He still watched her now. Many of the guests had retired, and the ladies of their group now surrounded her. He saw the smile finally fall away to reveal the heaviness the evening had left upon her.

God, she had looked so afraid. He should have killed the bastard.

"Yes, darling," his mother came up beside Oliver, and Charles glanced at her to see the worry carved into her features as she, too, observed Anna. "You've had a trying night. We can handle the rest from here, there's no reason for you two to stay."

Charles looked from his mother to Oliver, their expressions sober. He was pretty sure Oliver got at least a punch in, too, as he, Gideon, Thomas, and Alexander had taken Perkins outside. And between the members of their powerful group, that excuse for a man was utterly ruined in all of England.

Charles nodded and crossed the ballroom towards his wife. "Ladies," he said when he reached the women clustered together, stepping in beside his wife and discreetly taking hold of her hand. "Thank you for your support tonight."

"Charles, you needn't thank us," Amelia replied genuinely. "We are a family."

He agreed wholeheartedly with the duchess and gave her a small smile.

"Anna," he turned to her. "Let us retire and leave the rest of the evening for our family to handle."

His wife's eyes melted with such relief, he wanted to punch that bastard all over again for ruining her night. She glanced around the group to confirm they did not mind her leaving.

"Go, Anna," Genevieve spoke from her other side before she leaned forward and kissed her cheek. "We will see you both tomorrow for Christmas."

With that, they said their goodnights and left the ballroom.

Charles did not release her hand and had absolutely no intention to. They were quiet as he pulled her upstairs and straight to his bedroom. She didn't ask questions or mention the oddness of where he led her. She likely felt as he did – he couldn't let her go tonight. He hated seeing his wife cornered, looking terrified, even as she'd tried to hide it. He could still see it in his mind's eye, the memory one he knew would always haunt him.

Closing the door behind them, he didn't bother walking further into the room, which was lit by the flames roaring in the fireplace. He turned to Anna and wrapped his arms around her, holding her tightly and resting his head atop hers where she laid it on his chest. Her arms encircled his waist snugly.

"Are you alright?" he asked in a whisper.

"I am now," she answered into the silk of his coat. Then, she lifted her head, prompting him to do the same, and met his eyes. "Thank you."

The sincerity in her words stripped him.

He brought both his hands to either side of her face and held it firmly between his palms. His eyes bore into hers as he tried to sear the message into her mind, heart, soul.

"You are *my wife*, Anna," Charles spoke the words with conviction and vehemence. "You do not thank me for taking care of you and protecting you. It is my right and honor, and I will not fail in it. I promise you, no one will lay a finger on you ever again."

Her hands came up and held his wrists. She gave a small sigh, closing her eyes before pulling his hands from her face.

"I understand," she said, holding his gaze. "But there are still other things between us that I would like to understand, as well, Charles."

"Like what?" he asked.

"Like everything," her voice choked on the last word, and his heart cracked seeing the sheen of tears in her eyes. "Please. Can you please tell me what has been going on between us all these weeks, months, years? I don't understand." She dropped her forehead to his chest, his arms wrapping around her again instinctively as she continued, speaking to the floor. "These last two weeks have been wonderful, but there is still a chasm in our relationship. A lack of intimacy. Part of me cannot stop fearing that things will return to how they were before. Please," she lifted her head again to look at him. "Help me understand."

# CHAPTER 37

## ANNA

*A*fter everything that had happened this past month culminating with this night, Anna felt beyond faith, hope, assumptions, beliefs. She needed stability. Standing there in this room that brought her peace, one she'd been in so rarely. Looking up at the husband that was, just as he said, her whole life. She needed things to be sure.

His gaze was soft on hers, his expression pained. The way it had been the last time he'd seen her sadness overwhelming her to the point of tears.

Charles bent down and kissed the top of her head, keeping his lips pressed against her as he whispered, "Of course." Then, he stepped away from her, taking her hand again and pulling her towards the chairs by the fireplace. He let go of her there and went to the small table beside his wardrobe, which held an array of crystal decanters full of dark liquids in varying shades. She took one of the seats as he selected one, poured the contents into two tumblers before stoppering the bottle and bringing the glasses back to where she sat. He handed one to her before sitting down.

Anna took a small sip and felt the liquor burn through her

mouth and down her chest, followed by a warmth spreading outwards from its path. Oddly, that single sip made her feel better after the madness of the evening.

"I am in love with you, Anna," Charles derailed all her thoughts with seven unexpected words. He stared into the fire, holding his glass between his palms, not bothering to drink it. "I think I have been for a very long time. I don't know when it happened. I know I've loved you since I was ten years old. In an innocent, childish sort of way. You were always so sweet, so perfect, so... *mine*. When that transformed into the love I bear for you now, I do not know. It just morphed into it. The way you grew up, the way I grew up. My love grew up, too."

He paused to take a rather large drink from his glass. She didn't speak. Couldn't speak. She watched as he lowered the etched tumbler, eyes still unwavering as he talked to the flames.

"And I hated you for it," he confessed, the words a knife slipping between her ribs. "When our marriage was first arranged, I didn't really understand it. I just knew I was being made to do something. Like so many things in my life, I did not have a choice. Already at ten, everything had been planned for me, and this was yet another item in the growing list. The older I became and understood what a marriage between us meant, the choice that had been stripped from me, from *us*, the more resentful I became. And whenever I saw you, you were a reminder of my stolen choices. Never mind that you were robbed, too; I simply had nowhere else to direct my grievances, so I directed them at you. If our parents were going to force me to marry you, I would, but that did not mean I had to be close to you. It became my way of punishing them, punishing you, punishing me for what I could not control.

"And then you were just so lovely," he continued, his voice growing warm. "You were always the loveliest, most beautiful thing in my world. And that just made me bitter, somehow. Like you were conspiring to take away yet another choice from me. I didn't choose to love you, admire you, want you above all others. I just *did*. How could I not? You are perfect." He looked at her then, something helpless shining in his light blue eyes. "I was always half mad whenever I was near you. My emotions a mess of contradictions I could never make sense of with you near.

"All the more reason to keep my distance from you, I thought," his gaze returned to the fire. "Somewhere along the way, the stubbornness, self-righteousness became a habit I could not break. It wasn't about you. Hell, it wasn't even about me. It just became this thing – this thing that I had been holding on to so desperately for so long that I did not know how to let go. It felt like I'd lose everything if I let go of it. I've wanted to, Anna," he turned to her. "For so long, especially this past year, I've wanted to let go of it. To be with you, laugh with you, live with you, love you, but I no longer knew how to exist or *be* without it."

He shook his head, mostly to himself, his drink forgotten where it hung from his elegant fingers. Hers, too, was just a thing for her to clutch as she absorbed his words. She couldn't feel it, the crystal in her hand or even the heat from the fire. She couldn't feel anything except the racing of her heart and the impact of his words.

"But I loved you. I am so desperately in love with you. You are the love of my whole entire life. And it was killing me to see how you were hurting. I had convinced myself that we could go on as we had been, keeping our distance. But I couldn't do it anymore. I couldn't hurt you or myself anymore by staying away from you. You cannot fathom the regret I feel for the mistakes I made, for the ways I have neglected you."

He stopped, their gazes still fixed on each other, as the silence echoed between them in the wake of everything he finally unburdened. It all made sense now. Hearing him explain it.

Except there was still one thing....

"I understand," she told him, her tone soothing. "But why, if you no longer wanted distance between us, why does it still exist?"

Charles blinked softly, comprehending what she asked. "You mean why haven't we made love?"

"Yes," there was no reason to be embarrassed about it. "I know we shared some wonderful intimacies just here," she looked down at the floor where he had spread her out. "But you will not be with me beyond that, even with my asking for it. I recognize that you are still not ready, but I'd like to understand why if you'll let me."

He breathed out through pursed lips and leaned back in his seat, lifting his glass to his lips for a sip before speaking. "You understand my damn near dependence on the distance between us? That I did not know any other way or how to end it, even when I was desperate to?"

Anna nodded, the truth of his admission easing something inside her.

"I must confess to similar flaws in this regard," he said, not quite making sense. "After eighteen years of distance and then the first few weeks of our marriage, I wanted to heal the history between us before we were finally together. I believed it the right way to proceed to strengthen us and our marriage."

The final piece of the puzzle finally snapped into place in Anna's mind. Her lips parted as she thought back through the past weeks, the shift in his attentions, the promises he made. It all made sense now. He wasn't ready because he strove for perfection.

Her intelligent, brilliant husband was an idiot.

She started to laugh. It started out as a disbelieving chuckle, but within moments, she had her face in her hand and moisture gathering at the corners of her eyes. Everything of what he told her made sense in the silliest and sweetest of ways.

"What is so funny?" Charles asked, a smile tugging at his lips as he watched her reaction.

"Charles," she shook her head, placing the tumbler on the table between them while she wiped at her eyes. "How were we ever going to heal if you never told me any of this?"

She didn't give him a chance to answer as she stood up and took the three steps over to him. Taking the glass from his hand, as well, she placed it next to hers, before sitting across his lap. His arms immediately wrapped around her waist as she draped hers around his shoulders.

"I never said I was intelligent," he admitted, his voice low and smooth.

Anna shook her head, smiling warmly. "You are absolutely brilliant, Charles, but for some reason, you really are rather foolish with regard to us."

"I seem to have been that way for quite some time," he agreed.

"I have been exceedingly foolish, too," she told him, looking at him like the wonder he was in her world. "We both should have erased the distance between us sooner. We both should have been less afraid. And I should have told you much, *much* sooner, too, that I am in love with you. You are my husband and the love of my whole life," she repeated his words back to him, eyes unwavering from his steady gaze. "And I have loved you and will love you all the days of my life. You have been a part of me from my very first memory. And you will be a part of me when all I am is a memory. I love you."

Then she kissed her husband with all the love and tenderness that filled her body and soul for the man that was the other half of her life.

# CHAPTER 38

## CHARLES

*C*harles felt like his heart was open and bare before his wife, and the way she kissed him now soothed the turmoil that had lived like a permanent resident within it. Her kiss was sweet and intense at the same time. Loving and passionate. She loved him. His wife, this beautiful, perfect woman was in love with him, and it felt like his life had sense and meaning as it never had before.

He kissed her back and felt his blood stir immediately with the power she held over him. Her soft lips, the gentle strokes of her tongue, her floral scent. He was surrounded by her, and his body reacted. His grip grew firmer where he held her waist, one hand caressing up her spine as he deepened the kiss. Her fingers settled into his hair at the base of his skull as she responded.

Anna pulled back, her hooded eyes finding and holding his. "Charles," she whispered in a voice huskier from her arousal. His cock hardened further at the sound. She swallowed before finishing what she wanted to say. "Charles, I don't want to wait anymore."

Neither did he.

Reaching up, he cupped his wife's face. She was breathtaking, and he still could not believe she was his.

"I love when you look at me like that," she whispered.

"Like what?" His eyes dropped to those unique lips, wanting to taste them again.

"Like you worship me," she told him. "Adore me. Are devoted to me."

He met her eyes. Let her see the truth in them.

"I do, wife. I am." And then he leaned forward and placed a chaste kiss on those full lips before moving to stand. She understood and let him up.

Charles took one of her hands and pulled off the glove before moving to the other one and doing the same. Placing the lengths of silk on the table, he took his wife's hand, skin to skin, and led her to their bed, stopping beside it.

When he turned to her, he didn't have the chance to make the next move as Anna's hands pushed off his coat then went straight to his cravat and began untying it. He smirked as he started in on the many pins and baubles decorating and holding her auburn hair.

"I love your hair," he murmured as he worked to unleash it. "I want to see it down and flowing always."

She smiled, clearly pleased, as she moved to the buttons of his waistcoat. "You know I can't very well do that."

He chuckled, finally getting the last of the pins out while she pulled his shirt out of his breeches and began unbuttoning it. "You can at home," he answered, collecting the hair adornments in one hand so he could run the other through her long red locks.

"I cannot," she looked at him in mock indignation, and he laughed.

"Well, how about in here?" he suggested as she finished the buttons and began pushing all his layers now open off his shoulders to meet his coat and cravat on the floor. "I want to see this red silk spread out across our pillows."

"Only if you stay like this in here," she said in a breathless voice as his clothes fell to the floor and he was bare from the waist up. Her eyes were fixed to his torso, and she lifted one hand to trace the ridges of his muscles and splay her fingers in the blonde dusting of his hair. Her touch left a fire burning along him in its wake.

He was filled with a new sense of masculine pride as she admitted how much she desired his body. He had recognized it when she saw him naked before, but it felt amazing to hear it, too.

"That hardly seems fair," he turned around to drop the pins onto the table beside his bed before facing her again. "We need to level things out a bit more," his voice was low and seductive, and she visibly shivered in response.

He gently gripped her upper arms and urged her to face the door. When she complied, he brushed her red silk mane over one shoulder, letting his fingers trail across her skin before he began pulling at the ties of her dress. Making quick work of it, it dropped to the floor, and she turned to him again and reached for his breeches while he worked to divest her of her stays.

"You could be naked in here all the time," he offered, his voice rumbling out of his chest.

"That seems even less fair," she countered.

"There was that wicked little nightgown you wore for me." He wondered if he should tread more carefully, not reminding them of the past in this moment, but fuck, her body in that thin piece of silk.... His cock twitched at the memory as she unsheathed it from his clothing.

He pulled at the rest of her clothes, letting them fall to the floor.

"Did you like it?" she asked, meeting his eyes with curiosity and hope.

He swallowed and licked his lips before telling her honestly, "The memory of you in that nightgown has haunted me every day and every night since I saw you in it. I hope to see it again soon."

Anna grinned. "There may be a distinct possibility."

They stood before each other naked once more, eyes admiring and hungry. She was still devouring him with her gaze when he cupped her face between his palms. Her crystal eyes met his, and he murmured, "I love you, Anna."

He felt, more than heard, her contented exhale as he leaned down and kissed her. Her arms went around his waist as she stepped into him, bringing their bodies flush together. It was like a match. Like the calm, simmering heat and desire between them thus far tonight immediately boiled over at the feel of her naked body against his, and he needed to consume her before he lost his mind.

# CHAPTER 39

## ANNA

*A*nna was full of nervous, buzzing energy. She could feel Charles's hunger in the way he kissed her, the way his hands held on to her and moved over her like she was the one solid thing in a sea of crashing waves. Before she could move her hands over him again like she wanted, he bent down and scooped her up into his arms, dislodging her hold around his waist, all without breaking their kiss.

She held onto his shoulders, the heat within her simmering along her skin and nerves, her body growing more sensitive and aroused by his display of strength as he lowered her down gently in the center of the bed, her head resting against the pillows. He covered her body with his own, and her already pounding heartbeat became positively erratic as he rested his forearms on either side of her head and kissed her madly. She drowned in him. His weight, his scent, his kiss, his touch. Her body softened and melted, heat gathering in her core as she grew ready for him.

She couldn't stop touching him. His skin was hot velvet beneath her palms. She stroked down his chest, loving the feel of his solid strength against her and the rough feel of his hair.

Then, she moved up the smooth firmness of his back, across his broad shoulders that covered her, and down his arms.

He shifted slightly, leaning on one arm while he trailed his other hand along her skin. He caressed down the length of her before cupping her breast, which ached for his attention. She moaned as he satisfied one of the many demands her body pounded through her. When his thumb brushed over her nipple, the feeling was so intense, she had to pull her lips away from his to gasp.

Charles kissed her neck and began moving down her body, but she stopped him before he could make it past her clavicle. "No, Charles," she couldn't recognize her own voice. He looked up at her with such irrational hunger in his eyes, she almost whimpered at the sight.

"What's the matter?" he asked in a rough voice.

"I do not want that right now."

His brow furrowed, and she noticed something like vulnerability flit across his face. "Did you not like it? I thought you did."

"I loved it," she told him honestly. "And I'd like it again tonight, if you don't mind. But I have waited almost a month for you to make love to me. I will not wait a second longer, even for that."

The smile that split her husband's face was almost devious, and he had never looked more handsome and wicked.

"As you wish, wife," he whispered, settling atop her again. His mouth found hers, tongue seeking, probing, consuming. Her hands wrapped around his back, clutching him to her as he used his knees to part legs. He nestled between her thighs like he was meant to be there, fitting her perfectly.

Charles pulled one of her hands from his body and held it in his, interlacing their fingers as he pinned it next to her head. He broke their kiss, rubbing their noses against one another softly, before resting his forehead against hers. He reached his free hand down to run the tip of his cock along her slick folds before shifting his hips slightly and entering where she craved him most. She gasped, her breath coming out in short bursts as he stretched her in the most exquisite way. He shifted a bit more, moving further into her heat, and they both groaned.

"Fuck," he grit out through his teeth.

"Are you alright?"

"It feels too good."

He stayed paused there for another moment before he pushed in further, and this time, it caused something to pinch inside her. Her sharp intake of breath made him lift his head from hers, his eyes looking half crazed, yet still overflowing with warmth and love. He brought the hand not holding hers to her face and brushed back the hair clinging to her forehead. He didn't speak, just kept his light blue eyes, full of hunger and tenderness, on hers as he shifted his hips again and seated himself fully, the pinch within her turning sharp, making her squeeze his hand hard as they finally, *finally* consummated their marriage.

Charles started to move properly, shifting in and out of her in long, slow, perfectly measured strokes, and quickly, the discomfort dissolved into a haze of her own madness. She clung to him as each thrust of his hips stole away her sanity.

"Oh, God," she moaned, as she felt everything slipping. "Charles, oh, God."

This was so much more than what they'd done before. The shape and feel of him inside her drove her body purposefully, unerringly to her climax, and it felt *so good*. The heat built and built within her, and she felt herself losing her grasp on reality as her entire life focused in on the way he stretched her, the friction of his movements, the spot he hit with each thrust.

"Charles," she moaned loudly, her body starting to tremble, her hand clutching his while the other moved to fist the sheet below her.

"Look at me," his already deep voice was deeper and rougher still.

Anna hadn't even noticed she'd closed her eyes. She'd forgotten completely about sight as all her senses concentrated on the feel of her husband inside her.

She opened her eyes and looked at him. He watched her with such love, such passion, such wonder that her trembling became almost violent beneath him. He moved his arm down to link it under knee and pull her leg up. His next thrust was so deep, so insane, hitting a spot within her with such precision, she exploded. Her whole body arched off the bed as she cried out. Her muscles clenched down on him, and a deep groan pulled from his chest as he twitched inside her and followed her over the edge.

Her body went lax – looser than she'd ever felt before in her entire life.

Charles laid soft kisses along her shoulder, her cheek, her lips. He let go of her hand to cup her jaw in the tender way she knew she could no longer live without as they found each other's eyes.

"Will that do, then?" His words were teasing, but his face was serious and adoring.

She felt her lips curving up, a new vixen waking up and stretching inside her after a lifetime asleep.

"Hardly, husband," she encircled his wrist, turning her head to kiss his palm before nuzzling into it. "I need more."

# CHAPTER 40

## CHARLES

*I*t seemed his wife loved sex. And so did he. The way she felt when he filled her, her warm heat, her clenching muscles. Nothing could ever compare. They'd made love twice more that night, trying out different positions, pleasuring each other with their hands, their mouths, learning what they each liked together. It was novel, loving, intimate in more than just the act, itself, but the experience of sharing the newness with each other. He found it was also easier to delay his own release each time. That first time had taken all his concentration and more to hold on until his wife came. Luckily, she'd been rather quick about it herself, and once she did, the way her body had spasmed around him took away any choice he had in the matter, and it was absolutely perfect.

They lay now in the after effects facing each other, their hands clasped together between them. She looked sleepy and loose in a way she never had before, and he felt a fierce triumph bloom within him at the sight. His wife was spent. Because of him.

"I want more," she mumbled, her eyes blinking slowly at him.

"You're going to kill me, wife," he said, but also, that male pride compounded within him. "I need time to recover."

She grumbled softly, nuzzling into her pillow. He noticed how she inhaled deeply, breathing in his scent, and his chest warmed.

He kept watching her. He couldn't take his eyes from her, and every so often, she cracked hers open to look at him before closing them again.

"Anna," he finally said, his voice low.

"Hmm?"

"How long has Perkins been bothering you?"

Anna's eyes blinked open fully at his question. She swallowed, staring at him as if searching for something before she finally answered.

"Since the day of the family dinner," she told him in a quiet voice.

Regret slammed into Charles. That was why she had brought him up in the drawing room before everyone arrived. He knew after seeing how Perkins cornered his wife earlier that it hadn't been the first time he'd behaved inappropriately with her. It was clearly an escalation. And he also knew without having to ask that Anna hadn't told him because of how unstable their relationship had been thus far.

Knowing it didn't make hearing it any easier, though.

"He'd been overfamiliar," she continued into the silence. "He spoke about the discontent in our marriage up to that point. Then, he came the day you went to Boncroft Hall. Both times he'd confronted me in the entry hall and stood too close, spoke too directly. He didn't do anything overt until tonight, but there was still a threatening air about his presence," she spoke quietly, reflectively. "I can't explain how I knew, but I did. Then, tonight, I guess he thought it a perfect opportunity when I left the ball alone. I just wanted a short reprieve to check my appearance, but he followed me."

Charles felt the rage growing within him, stretching out from his pounding chest to the edges of arms and legs. His jaw clenched, hands shaking as his muscles contracted.

Anna's grip on his hand tightened, and she pulled it to her, kissing his knuckles and clutching it against her heart.

"Everything is alright now, Charles," she murmured, her voice and gaze soothing. "You found him and stopped him before he could try to harm me."

"He *did* harm you," Charles's voice vibrated with his anger. "You were terrified, Anna."

"Yes," she agreed with a nod. "But you were there, Charles."

"Too late," his heart clenched at the admission. "I left you an open target for the bastard and so alone that you felt you could not come to me."

She heaved a small sigh before she scooted closer on the bed, laying her free hand against his cheek.

"And I didn't tell you," she said in a warm voice that poured down his spine, calming and accepting. "I created an open target, too, holding myself apart. It takes the two of us to create our marriage, both the bad and the good. We've both made mistakes. Pushed each other away, kept ourselves isolated. We did not intend to hurt each other. Only to protect ourselves, not realizing we could protect each other. And we have spent long enough, too long, that way. It's time for us to move past it, leave it behind us and start building our life together. You didn't fill Perkins will his ill-intentions. You didn't force his inappropriate behavior. But you stopped him. And you will never allow me to be an 'open target' for anyone again, and I will never hide any discomfort from you. The past doesn't matter. All that matters is now. Now and the future."

Charles lowered his head to hers, closing his eyes and focusing on his breathing as he inhaled the light scent of flowers. She was right. As hard as it was, he needed to let it go. For her. For him. He would no longer hold on to bitterness, resentment, or regret. Because she wanted him to build and focus on a future with her. So, he would. For them both.

He kissed her forehead before moving back again.

"Very well," he smiled. He knew it didn't fully reach his eyes. He would let go, but it would take a bit of time and work. This was the first step. "Speaking of the future, when were you going to tell me you want children?"

She eyed him. He could tell she saw how he forced himself to move past the regret, that it wasn't coming naturally to him, but she supported him. She arched a brow and shifted the subject with him as she took her hand from his face and wrapped it with the other one holding his. "Did you think I did not?"

"Of course, I knew you did," he smiled a bit easier.

"Then?" she challenged.

"I did not realize how *eager* you were for them," he supplied.

"Ah," she nodded. "I imagine Genevieve told Oliver, and Oliver told you?"

He chuckled. "My clever wife."

"Charles," she said sweetly. "I very much want children. I have for quite some time."

"Is that right?" he asked, his body sparking at hearing the words straight from her lips. He rolled over her, pulling her beneath him.

"I thought you needed time to recover?" His marvelous wife was already panting. He could feel the heat of her as he nestled between her thighs.

"I am recovered," he ran his hands down her body, finding her center. "We have children to bring into the world, wife."

# CHAPTER 41

## ANNA

"Good morning, wife," the deep, sleep roughened sound of her husband's voice pulled Anna fully awake. She was smiling before she even opened her eyes, blinking to bring him into focus. He faced her, the sheets gathered at his waist displaying his bare chest as he smiled, golden hair mussed, pale blue eyes shining with adoration in the early morning light. His hand stroked along her spine as she lay on her stomach, head turned towards him. "Merry Christmas."

Anna closed her eyes, savoring the feeling of waking up to her husband. It was the best start to any day.

She opened her eyes again to meet his as she answered, "Merry Christmas, Charles."

Charles, her stoic, serious, outwardly cold husband beamed at her, and she had a clear vision of what her child would like on Christmas morning. Her heart swelled with joy and want. He leaned forward and kissed her. It didn't take long for the sweet good morning kiss to become heated. After all, they'd spent half the night making love, their bodies were likely almost fully programmed to recognize each other and the pleasure that came from the other. His tongue started seeking as she shifted towards him, aligning their bodies and hooking her leg over his hip while his arm wrapped around her waist and pulled her the rest of the way against him. She whimpered into the kiss, barely awake and totally desperate for him.

Charles lifted his head slightly, his lips still brushing against hers as he asked, "What do we have planned for today?"

"A closed family breakfast. Our friends will be joining, as well," she whispered, her breath coming out in pants. Her hands stroked down his chest, and Charles seemed to decide to multi-task while she answered, moving down her neck and planting soft kisses that chipped at her sanity. "The other guests are leaving this morning. Then...," she moaned as he shifted his hips to rub his hard length against her now throbbing clit while his fingers pinched and rolled her pebbled nipple. "Then, we'll do gifts with the staff before they have their luncheon, and we have the afternoon free."

"We'd best be quick then," he murmured in that intensely seductive timbre of his as he shifted his hips again, this time sinking into her easily. Her neck arched on a deep moan as her body stretched around him, and he took the advantage and latched onto it as they moved together.

Yes, it was the best possible start to any morning.

THE MORNING HAD BEEN PERFECT. They'd had the most wonderful Christmas breakfast with her mother-in-law, her parents, Oliver, Genevieve, Gideon, Amelia, Thomas, Lydia, Philip, Alexander, Jack, Emily, and Grace. It had been full and joyous. Laughter, conversation, and so much activity and love that Anna could not believe how happy and full her life felt. All the while Charles had snuck glances at her from where he sat beside her, his lips smirking, his eyes shining.

Since then, their other guests from the ball had departed;

they gave their gifts to their wonderful staff that Anna had come to appreciate and care for in the short month of living at Sinclair Manor; and then gathered in the drawing room for their luncheon and tea while the staff celebrated their Christmas meal.

Anna laughed and talked with her friends and family, watched and held Adelaide, George, John, and Guinevere as they bustled about the room, happy and playing with the occasional upset that their parents managed seamlessly. She hoped next year her own child would be in the mix along with Genevieve and Amelia's upcoming ones.

They were all scattered throughout the room. The men, including George and John, were set in a game of cards at the table by the window, while Prudence and the Dunhills sat talking comfortably by the fire. Genevieve, Amelia, Lydia, and Grace sat near them on the other sofa and armchair, holding a separate conversation and playing with Guinevere. Anna and Emily sat with Adelaide by the other large window, and Anna was aware of Charles's eyes watching her often. She, too, had trouble keeping her gaze from him.

Adelaide had just run off from where she'd been sitting on Anna's lap beside Emily when Genevieve, seeing that they had a semblance of privacy in the bustling room, left her conversation with Amelia, Lydia, and Grace, to sit on Anna's other side.

"You look deliriously happy," Genevieve whispered to her in a low voice.

She knew all their friends had been waiting, and likely probing, for the details on the obvious shift between her and Charles. She imagined a lot of the low conversations around the card table had to do with that, and that once Amelia, Lydia, and Grace had the opportunity, they, too, would be asking questions.

"You *both* look deliriously happy," Emily joined in. "I don't think I've ever seen Charles with such warmth in his eyes before. And he cannot stop looking at you," she finished. All three of them looked over to find Charles watching Anna, proving Emily's point, and started laughing. Her husband quirked a brow at her, amusement lighting his face, as Oliver elbowed his brother, muttering something, and the rest of the men joined in, likely telling him to focus on the game.

"I am happy," Anna told her friends. Now that her hands were free, she picked up her tea from the small table in front of her. Luckily, some warmth still remained to the liquid as she took a sip. "I thought it might not be possible for us, but we are finally very happy."

"And everything that happened with Perkins?" Genevieve's brow pulled down and anger filled her dark eyes, turning them hard.

"Was that the awful man from last night?" Emily asked, her lips twisted in disgust. Anna and Genevieve nodded before she continued, "I could have killed him." Her bright friend's voice and face darkened at the threat, and even in that, she seemed almost stellar in her darkness.

Anna chuckled as she watched her lifelong friend lift the golden rimmed floral teacup and take a sip. "You sound like Charles," she told her.

"Rightly," Emily burst. "How dare he corner and threaten you? Who the hell did he think he was?"

"Em," Anna reached a hand out to squeeze Emily's in her lap. "I am alright."

"I really did think Charles was going to kill him," Genevieve commented coolly as if Emily wasn't ready to cause a scene and go find the former steward herself. "*That* was a sight. He was so calm. It was rather terrifying."

"He's in love with you," Emily nodded, clearly still irritated, but moving on to the new topic the ladies wanted to discuss.

"Yes," Anna removed her hand, nodding and smiling. She was not one to show this much joy – that was Emily's forte –

but when she remembered that her staid, resolute husband was in love with her, she was sure she outshined even Emily's brightness.

"And you're in love with him," Genevieve observed, her gaze assessing.

"Yes," was all Anna supplied.

"Fucking finally," Genevieve sighed and leaned back on the couch, laying a hand atop her growing belly, as if she'd been working nonstop at getting Charles and Anna to admit their feelings and could now relax. That was likely the case for all their friends.

"On the plus side," Anna offered, shifting the topic once more, "I am fairly certain all of your combined efforts this past year brought Philip, Alexander, Jack, and even Grace more expeditiously into our group, so perhaps it worked out well." She drank her tea and her eye caught Genevieve's sarcastic expression over the rim of her cup, her sister-in-law eyeing her as if to say 'really?'

"That's quite the spin." Emily seemed of a similar mindset.

Anna pounced on the opportunity. She also needed to bring Genevieve, as well as the other women, into the loop so they could start scheming, and this was as good a time as any.

"I think it's more than just a spin," Anna said tactfully, depositing her finished cup on the table once more. "Without Charles and my need for all your support these months, Philip may not have joined our party so easily, or at all, and I do think he's become *quite* the friend to you."

Anna was surprised and beyond satisfied to see the color rising in Emily's cheeks. She glanced at Genevieve to see if she saw it, too, which of course, she did. Her sister-in-law rarely missed anything, and her eyes were now squarely zeroed in on Emily's face.

"He's been a friend to all of us," Emily, the bright, bubbly, enthusiastic woman replied lamely.

"Indeed," Genevieve spoke from where she still reclined. "I must admit, I've noticed his particularly close friendship with you, as well."

Obviously. It was Genevieve. What *didn't* she notice?

Emily rolled her eyes, but her cheeks remained brighter than usual.

Genevieve sighed from beside her. "Will we never get a break?"

Anna smiled softly. "Perhaps once we finish with the Davenports, sister."

# CHAPTER 42

## CHARLES

*F*inally, the card game finished, and Charles muttered a quick excuse, standing up.

"Yes, go," Oliver jibed, but Charles knew his brother was as pleased as everyone else to see the happiness between him and Anna. "You're ruining the game with your lack of focus."

"Newlyweds," Gideon muttered, smirking as he dealt the next round, leaving Charles out of it.

"As if you three are any better," Jack commented, watching the cards land on the table.

"I neither deny nor apologize for my obsession with my wife," Thomas said cheerfully. "Nor do I begrudge any man his passion. You go on being distracted, Charles, let this lot grumble amongst themselves."

"You're an idiot," Gideon said to his brother-in-law as he finished dealing.

"You aren't exactly an inattentive husband, Gideon," Philip pointed out.

"Can we please get back to the game?" Alexander said in a deep voice, and the group started their next round.

Charles stepped away, rounding the table to approach his

wife seated with Genevieve and Emily. They watched him with a quick mutter of something between them, likely not too dissimilar from the men's grumblings.

"Ladies," he said as he stood before them. "Might I steal my wife for a bit?"

"Aren't you a poor thief, indeed?" Emily replied with amusement. "Stealing that which is already yours."

"Just be sure to return her intact, Charles," his sister-in-law drawled.

Anna, meanwhile, had already stood and stepped to Charles's side.

"I make no promises," Charles quipped and looked down to meet his wife's crystal eyes. "I may need to hoard her away from you greedy lot."

"As if you could," Emily scoffed, unconcerned.

Anna actually rolled her eyes and wrapped her hand around his arm, and he led her from the drawing room, aware of every single person's attention on them.

"They're a nosy bunch," Charles muttered as he dropped his arm to take hold of Anna's hand instead.

"They've been worried," Anna reminded him.

"Obviously," he smiled at her as he pulled her towards the stairs. "It will probably be a few weeks yet before they're finally minding their own business."

"Speaking of which," Anna perked up as the thought reminded her of something. Climbing the steps, she didn't ask him what he was doing or where he was taking her, and that oddly pleased him. As if she just implicitly trusted him. "I think there might be something between Emily and Philip. Or at least, there *could* be something between them."

"Hmm," Charles considered the idea. The two had paired off quite often, but Charles hadn't thought anything of it, assuming it was simply a result of the existing couples within their group. "Do you think they are well-suited to each other?" he asked her, cutting through the upstairs hallway.

"I think so. There's clearly a close friendship blossoming between them. That's not nothing."

"Very true," he nodded. "And are you planning to conspire on their behalf, wife?" He smirked at her, pulling her into their bedroom and shutting the door behind them. He finally dropped her hand and crossed to the table by his side of the bed.

Anna stood fixed by the door, looking around. "Charles?" she asked, distracted by the sight of her dressing table by the window.

He looked up from where he'd opened the table drawer, following her gaze. "Ah. The staff shifted your belongings this morning," he shrugged, turning back to the drawer. "Your clothes are likely in the wardrobe, too."

He heard her light footsteps crossing the room and opening their wardrobe to check while he pulled out the box he needed and shut the drawer again.

"But it's Christmas," she said when he turned around, her hand brushing over her dresses hanging next to his clothes. "They should have been enjoying their holiday and relaxing."

Charles walked over and wrapped his arms around her from behind, loving the sight of their belongings sharing space together.

"They insisted, Anna," he whispered. "They've been just as eager as everyone else to see us happy together. I don't think Smith and Mrs. Jaspers intend on letting us sleep apart ever again."

Anna bit her lip, still hesitating. Then, she sighed, a smile tugging at her lips as she turned around in his arms to face him.

"It seems we troubled quite a few people, didn't we?" she said, wrapping her arms around his waist like she loved to do.

"More like everybody," he agreed, reaching up and cupping her jaw. He rubbed his thumb over her freckled cheek before placing a sweet kiss on her lovely lips. "You didn't answer my question, wife. Do you intend to conspire on behalf of Emily and Philip?"

"Yes," she smiled at him, completely unapologetic. "Will you talk to the men to work on Philip?"

"Of course," he answered without hesitation, leaning down to kiss her lips again.

She made a contented sound before finally asking, "So, tell me, why have you brought me up here after very rudely abandoning our guests on Christmas day?"

"I doubt they mind. But even if they do, it does not matter. I have a gift for my wife." He pulled back and lifted the small box he held between them.

Anna looked down at it before she released her hold on him to take it. She opened the lid, and he delighted in her gasp.

"Charles," she breathed. Her hand trembled as she lifted a finger to the brooch in the shape of a foxglove, tracing down the bright rubies, curves of gold, and studded diamonds.

He stayed silent, watching her, not needing to explain because he knew she understood. It wasn't just her favorite flower he gifted her. It was *their* flower. Foxgloves. A reminder of the day he finally realized he loved this beautiful, magnificent, unimaginable woman. *His wife.*

She looked up him. His breath caught as he noticed the glassiness of her eyes, and the love that she leveled him with.

"Thank you," she said in a low, vibrating voice.

The look in her eyes, the unreal beauty of her face, the love swelling in his chest....

Charles couldn't speak. He didn't have the words.

So, he leaned down and sealed his lips to his wife's.

# EPILOGUE

*4 months later*

"It feels so odd, being back in London but not at my parents' Townhouse," Anna commented, sighing as she stepped into the bright entry hall of Sinclair House.

"Now you are in your own Townhouse," Charles lifted the hand he held, kissing her knuckles.

She smiled at her husband. "I am."

"My dears," Prudence's happy voice called as she made her way down the staircase, approaching them. "How was the Lake District?"

"Mother," Charles stopped mid-stride, still holding on to his wife as he watched his mother descend upon them. "I thought you were staying with Oliver and Genevieve?"

"I was," she answered, reaching them. She lifted her cheek for Charles's kiss before leaning forward to kiss Anna's. "I *am*. William is quite the handful," she rolled her eyes. "Although, I expected no less, given how... exuberant his parents are." Before she had even finished speaking, Prudence had turned and led the way to the drawing room.

Anna caught Charles's eye as they followed her, both

thinking the same thing – the original handful in the family was none other than Prudence, herself.

Anna giggled, the sound still warming Charles down to his soul and making him smile.

"When shall we meet our nephew?" she asked loud enough for Prudence to hear a few steps ahead as they entered the pale walled drawing room. They crossed to the soft green couch across from the one Prudence had settled herself in. Charles waited until his wife took her seat before he moved to the fireplace and pulled the cord, calling for tea. Then, he joined Anna, taking hold of her hand again as he reclined next to her.

"Tonight, if you both aren't too fatigued," Prudence replied, eyeing Anna directly.

Charles's heart swelled with pride as he turned to his wife. She was only just starting to show, and it wasn't obvious through her clothing yet, but he loved the sight of their growing child.

"Not at all," Anna glanced at him, checking to see if he agreed.

"Whatever you want, wife," he replied.

Prudence grinned so broadly at his words, Charles had to actively fight not to roll his own eyes, but he focused on his wife's happy smile instead.

"How has this Season been progressing, Mother?" Anna asked.

"Well, I believe. I haven't noticed anything too scintillating to divulge yet, but I am sure your friends will share any details you missed."

The tea tray was brought in, and their conversation paused as Anna and Charles greeted the maid and asked after her and her family.

"You haven't answered my question, yet," Prudence said, taking the delicate china cup Anna held out with its green flowery design. It seemed to match quite well with the furniture in the room. Anna would be making this house her own, too, as she had Sinclair Manor before they left for their honeymoon, but she might keep this tea set and furniture pairing.

"What question, Mother?" Charles asked, taking the cup Anna handed him.

"How was your honeymoon?" Prudence, unlike Charles and Anna, had no qualms whatsoever about rolling her eyes excessively, and she did so again. "Did you enjoy the Lake District?"

"Very much," Anna smiled, leaning back against the couch and stirring her tea to cool it while she gave her mother-in-law a small smile. "It was beautiful."

"Your father and I went there a few times over the years," Prudence's smile was wistful as she drank her tea.

"I remember," Charles replied.

"What's William like?" Anna asked.

Prudence sighed theatrically. "As I said, he's a spirited one," she answered, speaking of her new grandson, who was only a few short weeks old. "He has dark hair like Genevieve, and Oliver's eyes. I cannot quite tell whose features he takes after yet, though his disposition is entirely Oliver when he was born. Unreasonably needy."

Charles scoffed. "Serves him right."

"How is Genevieve?" Anna asked in a worried voice after her sister-in-law, who she hadn't seen through the last days of her pregnancy. "Her letters say she's been well, but I don't think I will stop feeling anxious until I see her."

"She's doing wonderfully, dear," her mother-in-law's voice and eyes softened. "Truly. Motherhood becomes her, as does fatherhood for Oliver. Don't you worry anymore about her. You must look after yourself until I come back once William has grown a little."

"I am here, Mother," Charles said, finishing his tea and placing the cup on the table. He relaxed in his seat again and placed a hand on Anna's knee, unconcerned of the audience his mother provided. "I am looking after her."

"Mmm," Prudence took the last sip of her own tea, as well, before speaking. "I know you are, dear. But I don't know if I've ever told you, you can be rather useless sometimes," she spoke matter-of-factly, placing her cup on the table.

"You may have mentioned it a time or two," he deadpanned.

"He has been taking wonderful care of me, Mother," Anna said, her voice confident and warm as she handed her near empty cup to Charles and he deposited it on the table for her. She then held the hand he had draped on her knee. "But I will be grateful to have you with us again soon."

Prudence's gaze shifted between the two of them, and the relief they so often saw there since Christmas returned. "Well, I shall be glad to be here and add to my growing brood of grand-children." Anna heard the thickness in her mother-in-law's voice, but she cleared her throat quickly and stood. "For now, I should return to William, and I will see you both tonight."

Charles stood with her. "We'll see you out," he said, and Anna began to get up.

"No, no," Prudence waved them off, stepping to the door. "You two get settled and rest before dinner. William might be a newborn, but he'll steal any remaining energy you have, I promise you that. Stock it up, my dears." With that, she smiled at them and left the room.

Charles resumed his seat, angling towards his wife and taking hold of her hand again.

"Eventually, she'll get used to it," he told her.

"Used to what?" Anna asked, admiring her husband's beauti-fully long fingers woven with hers. She stroked her thumb over his skin.

"Us being happy together."

Anna laughed lightly, meeting her husband's eye. "If you say so," she replied. "Personally, I think it may take another eighteen years."

"No, not that long," Charles shook his head. "I imagine half a dozen children ought to do the trick, though."

"Half a dozen?" Her brows rose as she eyed him. "I hate to disillusion you, husband, but that's about two or three too many."

"Since when?" he kept teasing her. "I thought you wanted children."

"Children, yes," she replied. "A litter, no."

"Six children is hardly a litter," he said, wondering how long she would take him seriously.

"Charles Sinclair, you are teasing me," she accused, answering his inner musings.

"I am, Anna Sinclair," he nodded gravely. "I am happy with as many children as you want to give me. Starting with this one here," he reached his other hand out and rested it on her stomach.

"Good, because you will not have six," she told him determinedly.

"Up to four," he nodded. "I understand."

She bit back a smile, shaking her head. Then, Anna let out another sigh. "What shall we do until dinner? I'm not particularly tired, even with the traveling, but I am not so ready to get the house in order just yet."

Charles's lips pulled up into a smirk, his eyes glinting with that look that never failed to curl Anna's toes.

"I have a few ideas," he purred, and her pulse started quickening even before he leaned into her, burying his head in the crook of her neck and kissing along her skin. "How about I show you our bedroom, wife?"

The End

# ACKNOWLEDGMENTS

I have to start by thanking my readers. Thank you for reading Anna and Charles's story; for giving my books a shot; for sticking with me in this fictional world.

A team of people helped me turn my stories into actual books. Thank you to Kaycee and Maddi, whose feedback made this story into one worth reading. Of course, thank you to Luisa for this amazing, amazing, *amazing* cover. And thank you to Jane and the team at TorchLitInk for getting my books into the hands of readers.

And then there are a few people without whom my books would truly not exist at all. Sierra and David, thank you for always encouraging me and my author journey, and for the Bookery. Manu and Laura, thank you for always supporting me and reading these books (and lying to me if you actually hated them). Addie, thank you for being my writing partner, my sounding board, my cheerleader. And finally, my husband, thank you for always believing in me and my dreams.

## ALSO BY K.P. MARCH

### FOXGLOVES REGENCY ROMANCE SERIES:

*The Mistress* (Amelia and Gideon's Story)

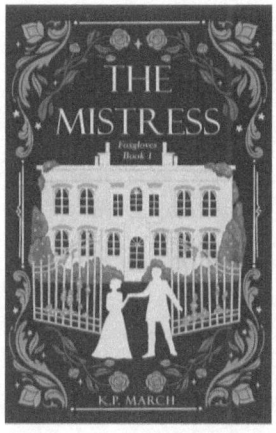

*The Gem* (Genevieve and Oliver's Story)

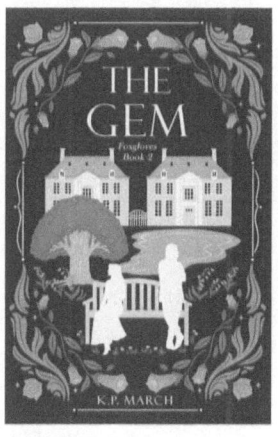

# ABOUT THE AUTHOR

K.P. March is a lover of literature, books, and the art of writing. She loves to lose herself in writing and reading books of dark romance, historical romance, romantasy, and fantasy, and she is an absolute sucker for happy endings. She studied Elizabethan Lit and holds a Ph.D. in Writing Studies. Originally from New Jersey, she now lives in the Cincinnati-area with her husband and three cats.

**Follow K.P. March at:**
**www.authorkpmarch.com**
**www.instagram.com/authorkpmarch**